KEEPING SECRETS

A SAM MASON K-9 DOG MYSTERY - BOOK 2

L A DOBBS

INTRODUCTION

Thanks for your interest in the Sam Mason Mystery Series! This series is set in small-town northern New Hampshire where anything can happen and playing by the rules doesn't necessarily mean that justice will be served. It features a small town police force and their trusty K-9 Lucy.

This is an on-going series with a completely solved mystery in each book and a lot of ongoing mysteries in the background. Don't forget to signup for my email list for advance notice on new release discounts:

https://ladobbsreaders.gr8.com

CHAPTER ONE

White Rock New Hampshire Police Chief Sam Mason studied the pile of resumes spread out on his antique oak desk. The steel-and-Naugahyde industrial chair he sat in let out a familiar squeak as he leaned back. The chair was a leftover from the post office that had once occupied the building where the police station now resided. The resumes were to replace one of Sam's officers, Tyler Richardson, who had been killed in the line of duty a month before.

A wave of guilt washed over Sam at the thought of replacing Tyler. He'd been a good officer who had been shot down when stopping to help a motorist. A random senseless act. Or was it?

Sam slid the middle drawer of his desk open. The sun's rays slanting in from the tall arched windows illuminated a small brass key with the number 317 stamped on top. The key looked just like the other keys in the drawer, but this particular key was no ordinary key. Sam and Sergeant Jody Harris had found it taped to the bottom of Tyler's desk after his death.

There was no concrete evidence that the key had been hidden there by Tyler. It could've been under the desk long before they'd moved in. The post office had left all their old furniture, and Sam and his crew had adopted it, leaving their flimsy desks and chairs back in the musty town hall basement they used to occupy. But Sam didn't think the key had been there when they'd moved in. Sam's gut told him that Tyler had hidden it there, which made him wonder if Tyler's death really was as random as it appeared.

Sam slid the key out. The metal was cold on his fingertips. He flipped it onto his palm and stared at it as if the key itself could clue him in to what exactly it would open. It was a small key, the kind that fit into a locker or post office box or safety deposit box, but Sam and Jo had searched every PO box, bus station locker, and bank in the area. None had been rented by Tyler. The box that the key unlocked and what was inside it remained as much of a mystery as the identity of Tyler's killer.

He tossed the key back into the drawer, his eyes drifting out over to the main street of town.

It was a typical New England town with a lush-green-grass common area and streets lined with brick and wooden buildings abundant with the fine architectural detail characteristic of the early 1900s. From Sam's desk, he could see a view of the mountains. The town was small, the area rural and filled with streams for fishing, mountains for hiking and skiing and fresh air. Sam loved White Rock and took his job as chief of police seriously. And, since he was responsible for the town's protection, he had to replace Tyler no matter what his personal feelings were. Tyler's death had left them understaffed, and an understaffed police force could hardly be effective in protecting its citizens.

His gaze fell back on the resumes, and he gathered them into a pile, revealing the worn surface of the desk. It was studded with staples and old circular inked post office date stamps. Apparently the previous occupants had used it for sorting mail. It was worn, but the honey-colored oak still glowed despite its age and neglect. Sam wouldn't dream of parting with it--it came in handy for spreading out his notes on the cases he was working. Right now, they had no cases, which made it even more important that he start contacting some of these applicants while he could spare the time to interview them.

Lucy, the German shepherd mix that was part of the new K-9 unit, shifted at his feet, and he leaned down, running his palm over her soft fur. Lucy had been a stray who had helped them solve a case. Now she officially worked with them full time during the day and came home with Sam at night. After years of living alone, he had to admit he enjoyed the company.

"Well, Lucy, what do you think? Do any of these candidates seem viable?" Sam asked.

Lucy whined.

"I don't really see any that stand out, either." Sam shuffled the resumes around and placed them onto the desk one at a time like a poker player laying out his cards.

"These two are a definite no." He pushed two resumes over to the corner, which left three. "I suppose I'll have to call these three in and talk to them. Might as well do it before we have any real cases to investigate."

Police work in northern New Hampshire towns consisted largely of feuding neighbors, lost animals, and fence disputes. Though, lately, there had been a large influx of drugs, and Sam had been battling the crimes that came along with that. He thought he had an idea of who was responsible for the drugs, but no solid evidence yet. An extra officer would be a big help. The department was small with just Sam, his sergeant and right-hand investigator Jody Harris, and a part-timer, Kevin Deckard. Once he filled Tyler's position, he'd have another full-timer on board.

He picked up one of the resumes. Gary Newport. Military service. Three years police experience in a neighboring town. He seemed like a good candidate, but somehow Sam couldn't get excited about it.

"Maybe I'll like him better if I talk to him in person. I guess I should have Reese start scheduling some interviews," Sam said to Lucy. Reese Hordon was the receptionist, town clerk, and dispatcher. She was attending the police academy at night and had hopes to join the police force, but until then, she eagerly did all the administrative work for the police department.

Lucy swished her tail back and forth.

Hiring someone would have its benefits. Sure, it would be a new person to train and get used to working with, but it would also leave him and Jo more time to look into what had really happened to Tyler. Finding time for that was problematic because the investigation wasn't exactly "official." Sam and Jo weren't even supposed to be looking into it--the state had already given up and had shoved the case onto the back burner even though the shooter was still at large. But Sam and Jo weren't going to sit still for that. Right now, they fit Tyler's investigation in between their other duties.

Tyler had been dedicated to his family and had lived with his mother to help with his disabled sister, Clarissa. Sam knew Tyler's entire paycheck went to Clarissa's medical bills. Not an easy thing for a twenty-eight-year-old young man to do. Sam could remember being that age twelve years ago, and the last place he would have wanted to live was with his mother. Sam had been married with two daughters at that age, but Tyler was single. Living with your mom when you were single could really cramp your style.

Sam figured he owed Tyler's mom, Irma, a visit to see how she was doing. So what if the real reason was to go through Tyler's things and see if he could find any kind of indication of what the key in his drawer might unlock.

He was thinking about the visit he and Jo had set up for later that day when a knock sounded on his door. Sam glanced up to see a shadow behind the textured glass window that sat in the upper half of the solid oak door. The door had also been original to the post office--only the gold-and-black stenciling on the door had been changed from Postmaster to Chief of Police.

"Come in." Sam welcomed the break from having to look at the resumes.

The door opened, and Jo popped her head in, her eyes falling on the stack of resumes and then up to meet Sam's. For a second, her wide gray eyes reflected Sam's own feelings. Guilt at replacing Tyler and determination to find out what had actually happened to him. And then she shifted into work mode.

"Got a call, Chief. Nancy Ritchie on Logging Road Number Four. She sounded frantic. Claims Bullwinkle just killed someone."

CHAPTER TWO

Bullwinkle was the White Rock town moose. He could be seen periodically in various parts of the town. Sometimes he'd been seen at the river, sometimes walking up someone's driveway, and a few times he even ventured into town and walked through the grassy common. He had his own Facebook page where people would post pictures of his sightings. As far as Sam knew, Bullwinkle had never killed anyone.

Sam hit the lights on the police-issue Tahoe. Jo rode shotgun. Her yellow smiley coffee mug was snugged in her hand, tendrils of steam wafting out from the fresh coffee she'd just made in the department K-Cup brewer. She had her polarized Oakley Standard Issue sunglasses on. Her hair was stuffed under a navy-blue cap with WRPD stamped in white letters on the front, a few unruly copper curls escaping out the sides.

Lucy had fought Jo for the passenger seat and lost. She sat on the folded-down seats in the back, her black muzzle resting on the console, her whisky-brown eyes switching from Jo to Sam as they talked.

"So what happened? Did someone run into a moose with their car?" Sam asked. He'd rarely heard of a moose killing anyone except unintentionally when they smashed through the windshield of a car after being hit, or if someone was dumb--or unlucky--enough to get between a cow and her calf. Sam hoped it wasn't a car accident. Those were usually messy. Trouble was, he often felt worse for the moose than the person.

"She didn't say." Jo sipped her coffee. "She was a little bit hysterical. Said something about it being out at the Donnelly camp."

Sam turned onto the dirt Logging Road Number Four. Decades ago, the paper mills had come to the area and devastated the forest by cutting down the trees. It had been a big operation and controversial. Sam remembered seeing old pictures of giant logs floating downstream in the river. And clear-cut forests that made an ugly scar on the landscape. They didn't do much of that anymore. The logging roads still existed. The land was still owned by paper companies. Now the paper companies leased the land to people who wanted to build camps. The Donnellys had such a camp.

Nancy and Bill Ritchie were waiting at the solid metal gate that blocked access to the road. The paper mills had installed them, and anyone who leased the land up there got a key to the gate. Nancy and Bill's camp was just north of Mike and Margie Donnelly's.

Sam eased to a stop. Nancy must have gotten control of herself--she was standing calmly next to Bill. For a second, Sam thought maybe she'd just overreacted, but the dark shadows of the turkey vultures circling overhead soon squashed that hope. It didn't take long for the birds to find a decomposing body, and they weren't picky about what species it was, either.

He rolled down the window and slowed to a stop. It being mid-June, the air outside was warm and fragrant with the scent of early-summer flowers. He could hear the silky whisper of leaves as the breeze passed through the trees, but the woods seemed eerily devoid of the usual noises made by birds and squirrels. Probably most of the animals were keeping away from the vultures.

"What's going on?" Sam asked.

"I was sitting on my porch just like usual, having my morning coffee, and Bullwinkle just came

11

barreling past. He stomped right through my tomato garden and took off like a shot. He was coming from the Donnellys'." Nancy glanced up at the vultures, her voice high and panicky.

Bill put his hand on her shoulder. "Nancy came running in. Said Bullwinkle was on a rampage. We've never seen him run like that."

Moose usually just lumbered along unless something spooked them. Bullwinkle was no exception. If the moose Nancy had seen actually even was Bullwinkle. Sam had a suspicion the townspeople's sightings of Bullwinkle were really several moose, but he didn't bother to correct them. He was glad there were frequent sightings. It meant the population of wildlife was still abundant despite the current effort of land developer Lucas Thorne to ruin most of the pristine land in order to build a big resort.

"Anyway, I walked down to the Donnellys' to see, because that's the direction he came from. Wanted to make sure everything was okay. It's only about a quarter mile down." Bill's face turned grim. "But when I got there..."

"What did you see?" Jo asked.

Bill glanced up at the vultures. "Something bad happened to Mike. I couldn't get a close look. All I could see was Mike lying on the ground, and the vultures..." Bill paused to take a deep breath. "Well, they were practically covering him. It was too late to help him, so I ran back and waited for you to come."

SAM AND JO left the gate open so the medical examiner and Kevin could get in. The Donnelly cabin was exactly as Bill had described. A pair of denim-clad legs were on the ground just beside the porch, the rest of the body obscured by vultures. Even outdoors, the putrid smell of death hung in the air. One red squirrel sat on a pine branch, chirping at them--otherwise, the only animals that could be seen were the vultures.

Bill and Nancy hung back in the driveway while Jo and Sam approached the body. The vultures flapped away as they got close, roosting in the trees and looking down at Sam and Jo, angry that they had interrupted their meal.

"Holy crap, there's hardly anything left," Jo said.

Lucy wore a dark-blue vest with K-9 Police stamped on the side in white. She sniffed at the body cautiously, working her way from the feet to what was left of the head, and back. She snarled at a vulture that had flown to the ground and was brave enough to try to venture too close. She went back to the hands then whined and looked up at

Sam. He made the signal, and she trotted back to his side.

"Is it Mike?" Jo stood at the head, looking down.

"I assume so." To be honest, Sam couldn't tell. The birds had made short work of the flesh that wasn't covered by clothing, so his face and hands were a bloody pulp.

The sound of a car in the driveway garnered their attention, and Sam turned to see the medical examiner van pull up. Sam was more than happy to turn the body over to him.

John Dudley, the county medical examiner, got out of the van holding a black crime scene bag and came to stand beside Jo and Sam. They all looked down at the body.

"Sure is a messy one," John said.

"Yeah, no kidding," Jo answered.

John squatted beside the body and got to work with his tools, measuring this and probing that, and then putting various things into plastic bags.

Sam took the time to study the scene. He had a good eye for details and was looking for some kind of a clue as to what might have happened. Near as he could tell, Mike--or whoever the body was--had been standing on the porch and then had either fallen or been pushed off. The camp was a rough work of old lumber and logs, as were most of the camps on the logging roads, which had been cobbled together years ago by the previous generation, who had leased the land in the first place. No one put much money into them, knowing they would be dismantled eventually if the timber company no longer wanted to lease the land. Mike's camp had a wide porch with no railings that was typical of the small camps in the area.

Sam didn't see any evidence of a fight or any kind of disruption, certainly nothing that would be caused by a rampaging moose. Maybe Mike had a heart attack and tumbled off the porch? Or maybe he'd been doing something by the side of the house and spooked Bullwinkle. Was it possible the moose got scared and gored him, and if it was, what could Mike have been doing that caused that to happen?

"You thinking what I'm thinking?" Jo asked.

"Depends on what you're thinking." Sam and Jo had worked as a tight team for about four years now, and they had developed a close rapport, each often knowing what the other was thinking. Jo was a good cop. A loyal friend. And someone he could trust to have his back. Sam didn't have a lot of people like that in his life.

"I'm thinking something's not right here." Jo pointed toward the body. "Look. The bottom of his feet are toward the house as if he fell off the porch backwards. How could that happen and why?"

"Heart attack?"

"Maybe. But what are the odds of that? And I doubt it was a moose attack. Last I heard, they don't come up on the porch and rarely attack people."

"Unless he was doing something to piss the moose off or she was protecting her calf."

Jo shook her head. "This body has been here for a while. Look at the vulture damage. How long do you think that took? When Nancy called, Bullwinkle had just run past her house."

Sam had already thought of all this, so he simply nodded. John, who was now going through the pockets, pulled out a wallet. He opened it up then looked up at Sam. "Mike Donnelly."

"Well, that answers that." Sam looked at the head again. "Unless that's not his wallet. But the other question is what happened to him? Nancy said she saw Bullwinkle run through her yard. Could a moose have had anything to do with how he ended up on the ground?"

John eased the shoulder of the body over so he could look at the back, and his face turned serious. He looked up at Sam then pointed toward the grass near where Mike's hip had been.

"A moose? I don't think so. Not unless they've started carrying guns."

JO SQUATTED NEXT TO JOHN. "That's a .38. Where did the bullet go in?"

"Hard to tell with this bird damage." John squinted up at the vultures. Most had flown off, but a few sat high in the trees, watching. "I don't see any gunshot on the torso, so my guess is the head, but exactly where, I couldn't tell you right now. Maybe not ever with what the birds have done."

"Let's not touch anything more until Kevin comes with the camera. I want a record of how the gun is positioned," Sam said.

John nodded and rolled the body back. "It was partially under his hip. See, the position of his hand right next to the hip hid it at first."

Jo narrowed her eyes at the hand. "You think he could have shot himself?"

"Either that, or the killer stuck the gun under him after he shot him."

Jo looked at the gun again then walked over to the porch and looked back, tilting her head to the right and squinting her eyes. "I suppose it's possible he shot himself on the porch there, then as he fell off, the gun fell under him. Hard to say for sure. We might need to do some tests."

Tires crunched on dirt, and they turned to see Kevin pull up in the department Crown Victoria. The Crown Vic was the other car in their two-car stable. Both had been painted dark blue and had the white lettering and police department insignia. Having only two cars could be inconvenient at times, but none of them minded driving their personal cars if they needed to.

Kevin got out with the camera and came to stand beside them. Lucy sniffed his pants and looked up at him until he took a treat out of his pocket and threw it to her. She caught it in midair.

"What happened to him?" Kevin thrust his chin toward the body.

"Not sure yet. Take photos all around the body. Check the grass for clues and casings. Make sure you get photos of the body as it is, and have John roll it so you can get the position of the gun before you bag it up. And snap the outside of the cabin." Sam walked onto the porch as Kevin started taking pictures of the body.

"What are you looking for?" Jo asked.

"Up here, folks look out for one another. There's a tight network of people that own these camps. Most are from down south, but some, like the Donnellys, live around town and have the camp for weekends. Since most people are from 'away,' neighbors check on each other's camps, so there's usually a sign-in board." Sam pointed to a small chalkboard that hung beside the door. A white piece of chalk duct-taped to a string hung from the side. "Kind of like an old-fashioned calling card."

Jo noticed the board was blank. "No one came to visit."

"No one that wanted their visit recorded, at least."

"Shit. I guess we'll have to go talk to Margie Donnelly," Jo said. She knew how Sam hated these notifications. She didn't like them much herself, but she'd been hardened to the news after what had happened in her own family. Though Sam seemed tough on the outside, she knew telling people about a dead family member affected him. She liked to think that her standing beside him when they had to tell a family one of their members would never return home helped a little.

"I mean, assuming this *is* Mike and someone didn't mess with his wallet. Either way, we can find out if Mike is missing and if there's been any trouble lately. We can't ask the family to make an identification on that." Jo pointed to the body.

"Nope. We'll use dental records. Maybe he can find a fingerprint."

Jo looked at the hands. They were pretty messy. She looked at her watch and lowered her voice. "We have a little over an hour before we're supposed to see Irma Richardson." The name of Jo's former coworker made her gut tighten. She'd liked Tyler, and even though he was ten years younger than her, they'd clicked at work. He was a good cop and a good person--that wasn't something Jo could say about a lot of people.

"Right. Let's go talk to Margie." Sam's jaw tightened. "That's the hardest part, telling the family. Sometimes they take it real bad."

Jo pushed her sunglasses up on her nose and whistled for Lucy, who was busy sniffing the tire tracks in the driveway. "They sure do, unless one of them is the killer."

CHAPTER THREE

Kevin watched Sam and Jo drive off in the Tahoe. So they were going to visit Tyler's mom? Sam's voice had been low like he was saying something he didn't want Kevin to overhear. Why were they being so secretive about it?

Maybe he was making something out of nothing, but it rubbed him the wrong way that he was often left out of whatever Sam and Jo were doing. Maybe their visit to Tyler's mom was just a social call, but Kevin had to wonder, especially considering the odd circumstances surrounding Tyler's death.

As a part-time officer, Kevin hadn't worked with Tyler as much as Jo or Sam had. He really didn't work much with any of them. The three of them had been full-timers and had seniority over Kevin, so they'd worked investigations together while Kevin was sent on the crap jobs.

Now that Tyler was gone, he was getting better jobs, and Sam had even offered him the full-time gig, but Kevin didn't want that job. He didn't need the money, not with the lucrative little side job he had going.

Thoughts about the side job sent a wave of unease through him. He still wasn't sure if what he was doing was the right thing. But it paid well, so he pushed those aside and focused on taking pictures. Bile rose in his throat as he snapped every inch of the mutilated body. He could practically feel the vultures' eyes drilling into his back as they watched him from the trees, waiting for him to be done so they could continue their meal.

He repositioned himself, lying in the grass to take pictures of the body from a low angle. The cool grass pressed against his cheek as he focused on the copper stain under the victim's head.

As the job of picture taking became mechanical, he started to regret his distrustful feelings about Sam and Jo. They had been making an effort to include him. Was he being overly sensitive? His father had always said that he acted too hastily, and now he was trying to make a concerted effort to think things through before reacting. It was probably just an innocent visit and they hadn't thought to include Kevin because Kevin had already been to Tyler's mom's house when he dropped off Tyler's things from the office.

He'd been surprised that Tyler's mom didn't live in a big place. He knew Tyler had moved in, and he thought maybe they could've afforded something better. Kevin's own house was modest but updated with all the latest accoutrements. The updates were because of the side job, not his police salary, though, and Tyler had the added medical expenses of his sister's muscular disease. But still, he couldn't imagine living in that one small bedroom. What Tyler had sacrificed for his sister had given Kevin a newfound respect for the officer. Too bad it was too late to tell him.

Done with photographing the body, he stood up and scanned the grass for any bullet casings, foot-prints, or anything that might be a clue. He wanted to do a good job to find a clue that Sam could use to solve this case. He glanced back at the body, which the EMTs were now loading onto a stretcher, then went back to bag the gun as evidence. Had the man shot himself? It seemed likely. With the body gone, he could do a better search of the area. He meticu-lously combed every inch, carefully taking photographs of the grass, especially the indented areas where the body had lain. He snapped shots of the position where the body had been in relation to the house and the woods, making sure he photographed everything just the way Sam would want.

As he worked, Kevin's thoughts turned to Tyler again. What if Sam and Jo were after something more than just a sympathy call? What if they were looking for the same things that Kevin's contact had asked him to search for?

Kevin had brought Tyler's personal things from the squad room to the house Tyler occupied with his family. He'd gotten lucky on that because it allowed him to search through the boxes without anyone getting suspicious. He hadn't found anything, though, except the thumb drive.

Too bad the thumb drive was blank. But he'd kept it anyway, just in case.

In case of what? His contact had been vague about what, specifically, they were looking for, and it didn't quite sit right with him. Kevin was even starting to question exactly who the contact worked for. At first he'd thought it was the FBI looking into suspicious activity they'd found on Jo and Sam. But now he was beginning to wonder. Did the FBI have that kind of money to pay out?

But if Sam and Jo weren't up to something, why

were they still investigating Tyler's death? He knew they weren't supposed to be. A separate task force had investigated it, saying their department was too close to the victim to investigate. He knew the investigators had ruled it as a random and unfortunate killing. But Sam and Jo didn't seem to agree. Which made Kevin wonder if the people that were paying him for this so-called information were right about Sam and Jo. If they were corrupt, why would they be sticking their necks out to make sure Tyler got justice?

Now that Kevin had worked with them more closely, he could see no indication that Sam and Jo were corrupt. In fact, they seemed to be good people. Honest people. People who wanted to make sure the law was followed and justice was done.

Then again, they did push the envelope when it came to procedure a little bit. He knew for a fact that Sam had looked the other way when Reese had done some things for them that were outside department protocol, and Jo had filled in Tyler's empty log from the night he'd been shot. She'd claimed it was so that Tyler wouldn't have a blemish on his record, but what if there was another reason?

He proceeded up onto the porch with the camera, taking pictures of the door, the snowshoes tacked up in an X on the wall, the old porch rockers with their chipped green paint, and the old-fashioned bicycles that leaned against the side of the cabin. He wondered, if Sam and Jo weren't the bad guys, then that meant the people that were paying him *were* the bad guys, and that made him wonder just exactly whose side he was on.

CHAPTER FOUR

Mike and Margie Donnelly lived on the north end of town in a big, sprawling fifty-acre farm that the Donnelly family had owned for four generations. Now that Mike and Margie were getting close to seventy, they didn't farm the land as much. Like many children of the old families, their two kids were now in their thirties and didn't have an interest in farming. As was the way with too many farms, the acerage used for crops had shrunk to one small patch near the house.

On the way out, Sam and Jo passed by a new hotel that was part of the resort that Lucas Thorne was building. Jo turned her head to look at it as they drove past. Sam didn't want to look. Seeing the concrete and steel where there should be trees and grass made him angry. Even Lucy was upset. She stared out the side window and let out a high-pitched whine.

"The Donnelly farm abuts this land, doesn't it?" Jo asked, her head still turned to look out the window at the passing construction sites.

"Yep."

"Huh."

Jo didn't say any more, but Sam knew what she was thinking. The same thing he was. It was no secret that Lucas Thorne was after the Donnelly farm. He'd been after folks to sell their land in this area for quite some time. Sam suspected that sometimes he did something a little more forceful than just make an offer for the property.

Both Sam and Jo hated the way the town was being built up. Hotels, golf courses, restaurants. The company Thorne worked for wanted to turn White Rock into a vacation mecca with a big resort. The beautiful scenery was second to none, and there were activities to bring tourists in every season.

Sam wanted the land to remain unspoiled, but right now things were working against him, not the least of which was the town mayor, Harley Dupont, who seemed to be influencing the rezoning of the town so that Thorne could build wherever he wanted.

The Donnelly farm was a typical two-story farmhouse. A porch ran along the front and on one side. A big red barn sat next to it at the end of the driveway. It could've used a new paint job. The barn didn't have any animals in it anymore. The fields, which should have been sprouting with new crops, were filled with weeds. A pang of sadness flared in Sam. It seemed that many of the old farms were going to ruin--or worse, being bought by Thorne.

They knocked on the door and waited for Margie to answer. Sam's stomach sank lower and lower, as it always did when he had to give this kind of bad news.

The door creaked open, and a small woman looked out quizzically, her eyes widening as she took in the police logo on Jo's cap. The woman wore a loose-fitting shirt and sweatpants and looked incredibly pale and fragile. Her silver hair was cut close to the scalp.

"Can I help you?" Her voice held a fearful note.

Sam didn't know Margie Donnelly personally, but he figured this was her. "Mrs. Donnelly?"

She nodded. "Yes. I'm Margie Donnelly."

"Sam Mason. Chief of police in White Rock."

"I know who you are." She opened the door wider and indicated for them to come in. "Is somebody in trouble?"

It was neat and clean inside. The furnishings looked

as if they'd been handed down through the generations, which they probably had. Margie walked unsteadily, leading them past the living room into the dining area, the wide pine floorboards creaking under their feet.

She indicated for them to sit at the mahogany dining table. The room was decorated with family pictures and old cross-stitches. There was a china cabinet in the corner filled with flow blue china. Sam recognized it because his grandmother had had the same china, and it was now sitting in a china cabinet inside the hunting cabin Sam had inherited from his grandfather and now called home. He noticed a few empty spots in the china cabinet. Did Margie use the china for everyday use? His grandmother never had. She'd said it was quite valuable.

Sam remained standing. It didn't feel right giving this sort of news while seated. "I'm afraid there's been an accident. At your hunting camp."

Margie sucked in a breath and grabbed the back of the nearest chair. "Is it Mike?"

"We think so, ma'am. You don't know where he is?"

Margie sank into the chair, her hands over her face, her shoulders shaking. Jo came to stand beside her, putting a consoling hand on the woman's shoulder.

Sam went into the adjoining kitchen and filled the stainless-steel teapot then turned on one of the gas burners while Margie composed herself.

"I was afraid something happened," Margie said after a while. "He went out to the hunting camp last night. He's been going there more and more by himself. He's been very depressed." Margie's eyes flicked to a bowl on the table, and Sam noticed several blue prescription-drug bottles inside.

"Was Mike ill?" Sam asked.

Margie shook her head. "Not Mike. Me. Cancer. I don't have long. Chemo helped for a little while, but now..." She shrugged and touched her short-cropped hair. Sam realized it was growing out from the chemo. "Anyway, the medicines help a little. But Mike knew there wouldn't be a lot of time. I was afraid he might do something..."

"Are you saying that you think he killed himself?" Sam asked.

"He said he wouldn't be able to live without me. I told him he'd be fine." Margie burst into tears again, and Sam waited while Jo poured the steaming water into a cup that had a teabag nestled inside. She gently placed a cup in front of Margie, who took it in her frail hands and sipped.

"So he went there last night. And he was

supposed to be back but never came back?" Sam asked.

"That's right. I wasn't sure if he came back and then left early in the morning. Sometimes I don't always know. You see, the pills knock me out. I have a high dosage for the pain. I was getting worried, though, but thought maybe he'd been home and I didn't notice. Things get a little foggy..."

"I see." Sympathy flooded through Sam, and he spoke gently. "Do you own a .38 revolver by any chance?"

"Sure. Mike has one. It's in a lockbox on the top of the gun cabinet over there." Margie pointed to a scrolled oak gun cabinet, an antique piece that would've made Sam's grandfather envious. It was made of solid quarter-sawn oak and had etchings of elk and moose at the top. Six shotguns rested inside. Some of them were also antique.

Jo went over to the cabinet. She was fairly tall and only had to reach her hand up to run it along the top of the cabinet. She pulled down a slate-gray box and brought it over.

"Who knows the combination?" Sam asked.

"Just me and Mike. And the kids, of course." Margie pushed the buttons and flipped the lid open.

The box was empty.

CHAPTER FIVE

"If he didn't leave a suicide note at the house, maybe he left one at the cabin," Jo suggested as they drove away from the Donnelly farmhouse. Margie had searched the usual places, but no note had been found. Jo looked out the window at the ugly resort looming in the distance. "I wonder if Margie will sell the land to Thorne now."

"Or the kids will. Sounds like Margie won't be around long enough," Sam said.

"Yeah. Sad, huh?" Jo took out her phone and thumbed something in. "Making a note to run down the serial number and make sure the gun we found is his."

"It's just about time to go to the Richardsons'. Let's swing by there and then go back to the cabin to look for a note," Sam suggested.

"As long as one of those trips takes us by Brewed Awakening. I need a coffee."

"You betcha."

Fifteen minutes later, they were pulling into the Pine Boughs mobile home park where Irma Richardson lived. Jo had a bag of jelly donuts in her lap and a Styrofoam coffee mug in her hand. Lucy was eyeing the bag hopefully.

The mobile home park was one of several in the area and probably the nicest one. Each trailer was well kept, with a nice grassy yard and a tidy tool shed in back. Picket fences, window boxes, and flowers decorated the neighborhood.

The Richardsons had a double-wide, and Sam parked in the driveway. The two of them got out, giving Lucy the command to stay in the car. They left the windows rolled halfway, and Jo shoved the donuts in the glove compartment just in case Lucy got adventurous.

Irma was happy to see them. Her eyes seemed a little less sad than they had at Tyler's funeral. The house was as neat as a pin. Irma had laid out cookies on a plate and had coffee and dainty porcelain teacups dotted with tiny blue flowers waiting for them. Sam's large hands made the teacups look like miniatures as they sat politely at the table making small talk.

While Jo could tell their visit meant a lot to Irma, she could barely pay attention. She was eager to get into Tyler's room so they could inspect the boxes and see if they could find anything that would lead them to the location of the box for which he'd hidden that key.

"We're getting along just fine, thanks to that donation from the police fund and the big deposit of Tyler's last check." Irma pushed the plate of cookies toward Sam.

"Donation?" Jo flicked her eyes from the cookies to Sam. What was she talking about? Jo didn't know of any donation from the police fund, and she certainly didn't think Tyler's last check had been anything big.

Sam gave her an I'll-tell-you-later look, and Jo snapped her mouth shut. But she noticed Sam also had a quizzical look on his face.

Sam scarfed down his fourth cookie and patted his lips with a napkin that had a fancy design embroidered in pink on the corner. "I was wondering since we were here if you still had the boxes from Tyler's things. We have some police stuff that we might've put in there by mistake, and we need it back."

"Why, sure." Irma pushed up from the table. "His room's just the way he always had it." Her eyes shone with sadness. "Haven't had the heart to go in there and clean anything out. Anyway, the boxes and everything are just the way they were when that other nice police officer brought them by."

Jo had forgotten that Kevin had been the one to clean out Tyler's things and bring them to Irma. She didn't totally trust Kevin. She had a funny feeling that he was up to something, and it wasn't just her imagination. Last month, she'd seen him going into a restaurant where Thorne and their shady mayor, Harley Dupont, were meeting, and he'd lied to her about being there. Jo hadn't said anything to Sam about it. It was in her nature to be overly suspicious, and she might be seeing something when nothing was there. She needed more proof than him being seen in a restaurant before she accused Kevin of something nefarious.

Irma led them down a narrow hallway into a small bedroom. The walls were a grayish blue, the twin bed had a blue bedspread, and there was a little blue rug next to it. Had Tyler lived in this room? Jo couldn't picture a grown man staying in the tiny room.

"I'm sorry Clarissa can't be here to see you," Irma said. "She's getting some treatments. Thanks to that big deposit. I know Tyler would be grateful for that."

"It's the least the department could do." Sam opened the lid of a box that sat on a small white desk.

"Well, I'll leave you to it." Irma turned and went back down the hall.

There were two boxes on the bed. Jo sat down on the bed and started going through one of them. It held the usual stuff-- pens, pencils, notebooks. She leafed through the notebooks, but there was nothing unusual, just handwritten notes on some of the tasks the police department was saddled with, like where the lights were stored for the town Christmas tree and how many fireworks should be purchased for the Fourth of July celebration and what kind of treats Rita Hoelscher's goat, Bitsy, preferred. Her heart weighed heavy as she looked at Tyler's writing and remembered what a stickler he was for jotting everything down. She put the notebooks back in the box. They weren't exactly confidential police work and didn't need to go back to the station.

"Nothing in here." Sam closed the box and eyed the desk. "But maybe Tyler wouldn't keep it at the station. Maybe he kept it at home." He leaned back to look out in the hallway to make sure Irma wasn't coming then opened the desk drawer and started riffling through.

"What was that business about a deposit and a donation?" Jo watched Sam open another drawer. He paused to look back over his shoulder at her.

"You know how some police stations have a fallen-officer fund that donates money to the family?" Sam turned back to the drawer.

"Yeah, but we don't have one of those." Jo looked under the bed. Nothing there but dust.

"Well, I might've helped that along a little bit." Sam deftly avoided eye contact.

"You mean you used your own money?" Jo stopped what she was doing to stare at Sam, but he simply shrugged and went to the closet. Her heart swelled. Sam really was one of the good guys.

He reached into the closet, his broad shoulders framed in the doorway. "I have plenty. But, the thing is, I don't know anything about this deposit in his bank account. What do you make of that?"

"No idea." Jo opened the middle drawer in the stand next to the bed. There was nothing inside but a bunch of hardcover mystery books. Tyler had been a reader? It looked as if they were well worn. Jo and Tyler had been fairly close and had worked together day in and day out for years, but there was so much she hadn't known about him, which made her wonder all the more about the circumstances of his death.

"We should check into that. Might give us a clue as to what really happened." Sam closed the closet door and looked around the room. "In the meantime, I don't see anything here that will give us any clue about the key."

"I was hoping to find a receipt from a gym or a bank or something, but no such luck." Jo tapped the laptop on the desk. "This is Tyler's personal laptop. I know Internal Affairs looked all through his work computer and his personal computer and didn't find anything, right?"

"That's right." Sam frowned at the computer then turned back to the two boxes. "Did you find any thumb drives in those boxes?"

Jo shook her head.

"And these are the three boxes that Kevin brought from the office, right? Seems weird Tyler wouldn't have a thumb drive to transfer files, doesn't it?"

"Maybe he used Dropbox or Google Drive or something. Maybe he did have a thumb drive and hid it like he hid the key." Jo carefully closed the flaps on the boxes then stood, taking one last look around the room as if she were saying one last farewell to Tyler. "Are we done here? I think we need to get to the cabin and look for that note."

Sam followed her out the door then turned back,

taking his own last look. His strong jaw tightened as his eyes roamed over the room. Jo knew that he was taking a mental inventory that he'd go over later in his mind.

"Yep, we're done. Let's get a move on."

CHAPTER SIX

Sam glanced up at the tall pine trees as he pulled into the dirt driveway of the Donnelly cabin. The vultures were gone, but not the blood on the grass or the bird droppings or the indentation where Mike Donnelly's body had fallen.

Inside, the cabin was typical of the northern logging-road cabins. It was small, with two bedrooms and a combined living room and kitchen area. The ceilings were low, the walls covered with knotty pine. It was furnished with cast-off furniture that was probably worthless a generation ago but now would bring a pretty penny down at Clara Weatherby's antique store.

Everything was neatly placed, down to the green-and-orange granny-square afghan that was folded along the back of the couch. If there had been a fight, it didn't happen inside the cabin.

Sam didn't see any note on any of the surfaces in the living room. He crossed the faded green-and-tan braided rug, past the small black cast-iron stove, into the kitchen. The countertops were yellow-speckled laminate, the stove an old two-burner white gas stove. The fridge was a miniature style with a rounded top that must've been forty years old, and Sam thought it was a miracle that it still even worked. But there was no note to be seen.

Lucy had come in beside him, and she sniffed around the trash barrel. Sam looked inside to see a plastic ham-salad container from the deli and an empty carton of milk. Dinner for one.

He glanced at the sink. Two drinking glasses sat on the drying board.

Jo came from the hallway that led to the bedrooms. "There's no note anywhere here."

"No, but check this out." Sam pointed to the glasses. "Why would Mike have two glasses if he was the only one here?"

"Good question." Jo spun around, taking in the scene. "But everything looks to be in place. If he did have someone here, then whatever happened to get him shot didn't happen inside."

"And just because someone might have been

here, doesn't mean they shot him. We can't rule out suicide just because there was no note."

"Can't rule it in, either. What we need to figure out is who was here." Jo opened up the crime scene kit she'd brought and took out evidence bags. "These glasses have been washed, but there might still be something useful on them."

Sam poked around the living room, looking for anything that seemed out of place. They couldn't actually call the cabin a crime scene yet. Maybe the autopsy results would reveal more.

Jo focused on putting the glasses into the bags and casually asked, "So you really gave Tyler's mom money?"

"Yep." Sam didn't like anyone knowing about his generous side. Why had he even mentioned it to Jo? He could have stayed silent and pretended it was tied into the mysterious deposit that Irma mentioned. But that would have been like lying, and he trusted Jo. She knew most everything about him, anyway... except for one thing, and *that* thing was something he hoped no one else would ever know.

"What do you think that deposit was?" Jo asked.

The deposit worried Sam. "I have no idea. Maybe it was nothing, but I think we need to find out. It could have bearing on what happened to him, but we have no idea what Irma means by 'big.'"

"Apparently it was big enough for Clarissa to get that treatment, unless you gave her a huge sum."

Sam remained silent on that one. "Well, whatever it is, it's not something normal. Which makes me even more convinced that Tyler *was* the person who taped that key under the desk."

"And if that's the case, you gotta wonder... *who* was he hiding it from?"

WHEN THEY GOT BACK to the station, Reese was sitting at her desk, her long dark braid pulled over one shoulder and a look that waffled between patience and agitation flickering across her face. She was young, still in the police academy, but she'd already proven to Sam that her superior computer skills were a great asset to the department.

Right now, though, she was negotiating with Bernie Cumberland about his sewer tax bill. In small-town police departments, one had to wear a lot of hats, and collecting tax bills and handing out licenses and yard sale permits were some of the many jobs Reese was assigned.

Her pale-blue eyes lit up when they fell on the white donut bag that Jo had taken in from the glove compartment.

Sam headed across the marble floor and straight to the K-Cup machine. The machine looked out of place in the old-fashioned building, which had been built eighty years prior and never been renovated. The building still retained the original marble floors, paneled oak partitions, and even the original crafts-man-style oak desks.

The best part was the old bronze post office boxes that had been left behind. Each box had twin dials at the top with gold numbers on a black back-ground. Below the dials, a fancy embossed eagle with a US shield on its chest sat proudly amidst fluted rays that extended to the edge of the box. Below the eagle, a small beveled-glass window let you see how much mail was inside. Sam couldn't understand why the postal service preferred ugly new metal boxes, but he was grateful. The old boxes still sat in their oak wall and now created a partial divider between the reception area and the squad room.

Lucy took up her usual station beside Reese's desk, watching intently as Reese explained to Bernie why he had to pay the full amount. As Reese talked, she slipped her hand into her drawer, took out a small dog treat, and fed it to Lucy.

Kevin was already at his desk, his head bent over paperwork. He looked up as they came in, stopped working, and swung his chair around to face them.

"The gun found at the scene was registered to Mike Donnelly," Kevin said.

"Oh, you looked that up already?" Sam was surprised. Kevin didn't usually do things without being prodded, but this time, he'd taken the initiative. Perhaps Sam wasn't giving him enough credit or utilizing him to his fullest. "Good job."

Jo sat on the edge of her desk facing into the room. She opened the white donut bag and tilted it out toward them. "Anyone want one?"

"I do." Reese came in from the lobby as Bernie exited the building. She hopped onto the desk beside Jo and peeked into the bag then stuck her hand in and pulled out a donut. Kevin and Sam declined.

Sam pulled a chair out into the middle of the room and turned it so the four of them were in a circle. He sat leaning forward with his forearms on his thighs.

"So did Mr. Donnelly kill himself?" Reese asked. Sugar sprinkled into her lap as she bit into the donut. Lucy had come to sit in front of Jo and Reese. Her eyes watched each falling grain of sugar as intently as a hawk watching a baby rabbit.

"Not sure. He was depressed, and we didn't see any sign of a struggle. It was his own gun," Sam said. "But the position of the body in relation to the gun seems off. And those two glasses in the sink make me wonder."

"Glasses?" Reese asked.

Jo pulled the evidence bags out of the crime kit she brought in. "We found two glasses in the kitchen sink. It could indicate someone else besides Mike was there."

"Or it could simply indicate that he used two glasses," Sam said. "It won't hurt to see if we can find any DNA or fingerprints on them, but they were in the dish drainer, so they've been washed."

Reese leaned forward eagerly. "But right away those two glasses are somewhat of a discrepancy. He might not have been alone, and we have to treat every unattended death as potentially suspicious until the criteria of a suicide is met without a doubt."

Everyone looked at Reese silently, and she explained, "That's what we learned in school, anyway."

Sam didn't disagree. He had a funny feeling about this case. Maybe it was his predisposition to think that everyone was up to something sketchy. Maybe it was just his gut instincts that he'd learned to trust after so many years on the police force. But he didn't want to put the Donnelly family through the stress of an investigation, so he needed to proceed with caution. He wanted to make sure there was cause to investigate first.

"I'm just glad Bullwinkle didn't have anything to do with it," Reese said.

"He probably was just walking in the woods and something spooked him. Maybe the turkey vultures. Or maybe the killer came back. Either way, those vultures did a number on Mike. That makes it hard to look for any of the signs one normally sees with a suicide, and until we can rule it as a definite one, we need to investigate."

"Vultures?" Reese looked down at the blob of jelly in her donut and swallowed hard.

"Doesn't take long to discover a decomposing body. But that means he must've been there for at least a few hours. Likely overnight, because it would take a while for the gases to accumulate. Turkey vultures can smell that gas miles away, and that's what attracts them," Sam said.

"It was hard to even tell where the bullet went in. We didn't even realize he *had* been shot until John found the gun under the body," Jo added.

Reese wrapped her unfinished half of the donut up in a napkin and put it back in the bag. "So you can't really tell where the wound was at the angle of entry. In school, we learned that a suicide will shoot themselves in certain places, and the angle is critical."

"That's right. Anything that wasn't covered by clothing was mutilated, so we know where he wasn't shot. Maybe John can figure out more. He could certainly figure out the time of death. Maybe he can rule out whether or not Mike could have shot himself. His hands were pecked up, and I don't know if there was enough skin left to find traces of gunshot powder."

"Heck, we couldn't even tell if it *was* Mike," Kevin said.

"Yeah, I don't want to subject the family to making an ID. How could they? His face was... unrecognizable," Sam said. "But he didn't come home, so it's a pretty sure bet he was the victim. And Margie said he'd been depressed."

"But being depressed is one thing, and especially considering Margie's illness, it seems natural that he would be. Killing yourself is another," Jo said. "While we're waiting for John to come back with more information, it wouldn't hurt to find out if anyone might've wanted Mike dead."

"Isn't it obvious?" Reese said. "The Donnelly farm is right next to all that acreage where Thorne is building the hotel. The farm is a perfect place for the golf course he wants to put in. Everyone in town knows that Mike Donnelly would never sell to Thorne. Margie wouldn't either, but I know she's very ill and doesn't have long to live. The kids don't want the farm. So with Margie gone, Mike would be the only thing standing in Thorne's way."

CHAPTER SEVEN

By the time the end of the day rolled around, they'd gotten word back from the medical examiner. He'd been able to make a positive ID through the victim's dental records and a partial fingerprint on one finger of his left hand that hadn't been mutilated. It was Mike Donnelly.

Around six p.m., Jo headed over to the local bar down the street from the police station with Sam. Sam's twin daughters were visiting from college, and he'd arranged to meet them there. Jo didn't want to impose on his family time, but he'd talked her into going. His daughters had mentioned they wanted to say hi to her, and since Jo had nothing else to do, she agreed.

Holy Spirits was a decommissioned church. It was a favorite hangout for locals, and its reputation for making the best burgers in Coos County brought in a steady flow of outsiders too.

The owner hadn't done much renovation, and opening the double doors felt like walking into the vestibule of a church. Even some of the original pews remained and were rearranged, facing each other with long tables in between. But that was where the resemblance to a church ended. The rest of the bar was dotted with round maple tables surrounded by captain's chairs. The lighting was dim, and it smelled of hops and grilled meat.

The bar itself ran the length of the back, where the altar used to be. Jo liked to sit at the bar because the mirrored wall behind it gave her a view of the entire room without having to turn in her seat, and she could see who was coming up behind her. Above the mirror, a colorful stained-glass window lit the bar with a dim ambiance.

The chairs at the bar were comfortable solid-wood swivel chairs with black-leather-cushioned seats. Jo took her favorite spot in the corner and ordered a beer and a basket of curly fries with a side of mayonnaise.

Sam ordered a Mooseneck, the local beer he favored. Jo swung her seat around to face the room, the heels of her black boots hooked into the rungs of the barstool. In the corner, younger people were dancing to the jukebox music. She recognized Sam's daughters, Hayley and Marla. Hayley was taller, with long, thick dark hair, Marla a little shorter and bleached her hair blond, cut in a bob. They spotted Sam and Jo and waved.

The beers came, and Jo swung back around, sliding an un-manicured fingernail under the corner of the label, peeling it back just a little bit.

Sam swigged his. "Do you think we should have Reese look into Tyler's bank accounts?"

"I don't know. I mean, I know she can be discreet, but this seems like it's big. What if Tyler was into something? I don't want her to get involved if it could mean trouble for her," Jo said.

"Yeah. I don't want to ruin her career before it gets started."

"What about Mick? Has he found anything that would indicate why Tyler had a big deposit?" Mick Gervasi was Sam's best friend and a private investigator they sometimes used to look into things that they couldn't look into in their official police capacity. Since they weren't supposed to be investigating Tyler's death, they had Mick doing much of the groundwork.

"He's out of town. Still looking into the grandson."

Jo nodded. Billie, the owner of the bar, was

approaching with the fries, and she didn't want her comment to be overheard. Billie shoved the fries at her with a friendly nod then turned to the other end of the bar, where someone was hailing her for a drink.

"I can look into Tyler's bank account." Jo dipped a fry into the mayonnaise then popped it into her mouth. She usually smothered her fries in ketchup, but using mayonnaise was "a thing" that the locals did, and after four years, she was finally trying it. Much to her surprise, it was actually quite tasty. Not tangy like ketchup--more smooth. Maybe she'd add mayo to her fry-eating repertoire more often.

"Sounds good," Sam said. The jukebox turned to a slower song, and Hayley and Marla rushed over to Sam. They greeted Jo like an old friend as they squeezed in on either side of their father, brimming with energy, their faces happy and flushed from dancing.

Jo's chest constricted as she watched Sam and his daughters. Seeing the look of joy on his face as he hugged each one of them hammered home the fact that she had no one.

She'd never married. Never had kids. Probably because of what had happened when she was young. Her early childhood had been wonderful, but when her sister had disappeared, everything had changed.

Her parents had turned into emotional zombies, and life had never been the same. She hadn't talked to her father in decades, her mother had died of grief, and her only remaining sister had turned to drugs.

Hayley glanced at Jo's beer. "Can I buy you another?" She winked at Jo, and Jo's heart warmed at the secret that passed between them.

When Jo had first come to White Rock, the twins had been in high school. On one of her regular rounds, she'd caught Hayley in a car with an older boy out at the lookout point. Not only had their clothes not been where they should've been, but there had been beer in the car, and they were underage. The beer had been unconsumed, so they hadn't been drinking and driving. Jo had let them off. She wouldn't tolerate drunk drivers, but she didn't like busting kids that weren't causing any real trouble. Hayley had begged her not to tell Sam, and Jo never had.

The shared secret made Jo feel as if she was part of something, and it reminded her of the way she'd felt all those years ago when her family was still a real family.

Jo nodded, and Hayley signaled Billie for a refill, which Billie promptly placed next to the beer Jo was currently working on. She'd managed to drink three quarters of it and peel off half the label, which now sat in a soggy pile on the bar beside the bottle. Hayley and Marla were still too young to drink, but apparently Billie didn't mind taking their money for Jo's beer. It might not have been quite legal, but since Sam was probably really the one paying, no one would complain.

The jukebox started up again, and the girls turned to Sam. "One more dance, Daddy, and then we'll go out to eat."

Marla looked over Sam's shoulder at Jo. "Daddy's taking us to The Chophouse for steak. You want to come?"

Jo wouldn't dream of imposing. "Sorry. Can't, but thanks for the invite."

The girls hurried off. Jo finished her first beer and started on the second, drinking more slowly this time. One and a half was her limit when she was driving.

"Hey, there's Kevin over there. I hardly ever see him come in." Sam jerked his chin toward the corner, and Jo looked to see Kevin talking to someone who was seated at one of the tables. She didn't know who they were, but they look to be about Kevin's age. Probably a friend. He glanced up and caught her eye.

"We should invite him to join us." Jo motioned for him to come over even though she wasn't sure if she actually wanted Kevin to join them. She still had a funny feeling about him, but maybe that was because she hadn't really given him a fair chance.

"Hey guys, I just dropped off some treats at the station for Lucy and stopped in for a quick one. Lucy really likes those bacon treats, and you can only get them down at Grovesner's over in Colebrook." Kevin stood in front of them, looking as if he wasn't sure if he should stay or not.

Sam gestured to the seat next to him. "Have a seat."

Kevin sat, and the three of them faced forward, their elbows on the bar. "Did you talk to the Donnelly family and give them the news that the medical examiner made a positive ID?"

Sam shook his head. "Gonna go there first thing tomorrow. I think they already knew it was him. I mean, he was missing, so where else would he have been?"

Kevin nodded. "Still hard hearing it for sure."

"Yeah."

Jo pushed the basket of fries toward Kevin. "Want one?"

"No, thanks. So do you guys still think it was a suicide?"

Jo had been thinking about that all afternoon. She was suspicious by nature, especially after what she'd seen happen in the investigation of her sister's disappearance. She knew people weren't always what they claimed to be. And she knew people kept deep, dark secrets.

In college, she'd studied psychology and was somewhat of an expert in human behavior. She was hoping Mike's kids would be there when they went to tell Margie about the positive ID. She wanted to see their reactions. Margie had obviously been upset, and no wonder with her current prognosis. It didn't seem fair to heap this on her, and it also didn't seem fair for Jo to be suspecting one of her children. But, as Jo had learned when she was ten years old, life wasn't fair. She had to consider all angles.

"Can't say for sure," Sam said. "We need to establish three things without a doubt before I'm comfortable and willing to rule it a suicide. One is the presence of the weapon at the scene. That one we got. The second thing is to be sure the wounds could have been self-inflicted. With the condition of the body, it's hard to tell. And the third thing is motive or intent. I'm not convinced that Mike was intent on taking his own life. Sure, Margie said he was depressed, but many people are depressed and they don't kill themselves. We need to see if he attempted suicide before, and need to dig a little further before we can comfortably close the case as a suicide. Don't you agree?" Sam glanced at Jo and Kevin, who both nodded.

"Yep. Needs a little bit more investigation, in my book," Jo said.

"Would you look at that asshole?" Billie stood with her back to them, her neck craned as she looked up at the TV over the bar. On the TV was Mayor Harley Dupont in a shiny pressed suit, his fake smile radiating out from the screen in a way that made Jo want to jump on the bar and punch it.

What was he doing on TV? Jo tilted her head to listen, and her ears were assaulted by Dupont's tinny voice listing off all his accomplishments as mayor. They were coming up on an election year, and Dupont was really pulling no punches to try to get elected. He'd even taken credit for getting the government grant that had allowed them to take Lucy on as a K-9 investigator. It had actually been Reese that had done the work, but none of them complained as long as they got to keep Lucy. The dog, who had been a stray with an uncertain future, had a good nose for police work.

"Bad enough we have to deal with the guy in person--now we have to watch him on TV too?" Sam said.

"Gotta wonder how he can afford commercials," Jo said as she picked at the label on her new beer.

"With the way he's swaying the rezoning laws to be in Thorne's favor, I wouldn't be surprised if Thorne was helping him out," Sam said.

Kevin's brow creased. "You think Dupont can be bought?"

Jo snorted. "Are you serious? You've seen how sketchy he is. And you know he's had a role in blocking some of the search warrants we tried to get on some of the drug cases that we suspect lead back to Thorne." Jo didn't actually know how much Kevin knew about that, but by the way he nodded, apparently he had been paying attention. Maybe he wasn't as much of a slacker as she thought. Maybe he was just naïve.

"I did see them having lunch together at Lago last month," Kevin said.

Jo angled her chair to look at him. She'd seen them having lunch together too, and she'd also seen Kevin come out of the restaurant at that same time. But Kevin had lied to her when she'd asked about it. Or at least she thought he lied. Maybe it had just been a misunderstanding.

"You eat there?" she asked. Lago was an upscale restaurant. No one on a cop's salary would go there for lunch, unless they had an ulterior motive.

Kevin laughed. "No. Not on my salary. But my

cousin works there, and sometimes I poke my head in to say hi. He flips me a few free rolls, maybe some leftover steak. Anyway, I was visiting him one day, and I saw Dupont and Thorne in there together. But I guess it makes sense that the mayor would have lunch with a prominent developer in the area, right? I didn't think anything of it. I mean, they were right there in public." Kevin sipped his beer thoughtfully, his brows pinched together. "You don't think they could be up to something together, though, do you? I mean, you don't think that the mayor is really on the take?"

"I wouldn't put it past him," Sam said.

Hayley and Marla came rushing back. They nodded at Kevin before surrounding Sam. "We're starving! Are you ready?" They glanced back at Kevin and Jo. "You sure you don't want to join us?"

Kevin and Jo both declined, and Sam threw some money on the bar and said his good-byes.

"Nice kids." Kevin hunched over his beer.

Jo didn't think Kevin was much older than Sam's daughters. "Do you know them from school?"

"No. I grew up in a few towns over, but I'm five years older than them, anyway." Kevin tapped his finger on his beer. He was fidgety, as if he wanted to say something.

Jo sat quietly finishing her fries, dragging them

through the mayonnaise dish to scoop out the last blobs.

"Is there anything new on Tyler's case?" Kevin asked finally.

Jo didn't want to let on that they were investigating. So far, Kevin had seemed a little taken aback any time he'd learned that they weren't doing things exactly within the confines of the law. "You know as much as I do. The state investigation didn't find much of anything."

Kevin shot her a sideways glance. "I didn't mean the state investigation."

"What *did* you mean?"

Kevin kept his eyes trained on his beer. "I know there's a lot of unanswered questions. I know that Tyler was out there helping someone and got shot. But how come they can't find the killer? The car was stolen, and there was evidence of drugs, but usually criminals that deal drugs and steal cars aren't that smart. Not smart enough to hide from a full investigation, anyway. Unless the state investigator didn't put much effort into it. In which case maybe someone else should."

Was Kevin suggesting that he'd be on board with looking into Tyler's death on the side? Did he know they were already doing it? Jo decided to play it safe. "Maybe. But we could get into big trouble for that."

"Right. I wasn't suggesting we do anything like that. But I do want to see justice for Tyler. So if anyone *were* to do that and they needed help, well..." Kevin shrugged. "Anyway, I gotta get going. Nice talking to you."

He slapped enough bills on the bar to pay for Jo's beer and fries along with his own and left.

CHAPTER EIGHT

Kevin clicked the fob, and his Isuzu, which was still parked over at the police station, chirped as the doors unlocked. The station was dark--everyone had gone home. Even Lucy was gone, Sam having taken her in the Tahoe, he assumed. Sam didn't leave Lucy alone in the station for long, and it gave Kevin a warm feeling knowing that Lucy was that lovingly cared for.

He got in his car and pulled onto Main Street, heading north. The car still smelled of bacon from the special dog treats, and Kevin's stomach grumbled. Maybe he should find some fast food or hit up a restaurant. But not the one Sam had gone to--he didn't want to look like a stalker if he ran into them.

His eyes fell on the town offices, and his thoughts turned to Harley Dupont. He knew commercials were expensive, but he thought Dupont had family money. Maybe he'd paid for the commercials himself, or maybe Thorne had helped him, as Sam and Jo had alluded.

Kevin knew that Dupont and Sam butted heads all the time. Dupont seem to have no qualms about rezoning rural land to commercial. He didn't seem to care about cutting down acres of forest and obliterating old farms to make way for Thorne's facilities. And if Dupont was in Thorne's pocket, how far would the two of them go?

Kevin thought about the envelopes stuffed with cash and cryptic notes that kept showing up under his doormat. He knew what the money was for-- information. He'd only been half telling the truth when he told Jo about meeting his cousin at Lago.

He knew Jo had seen him that day last month, and he'd panicked and screwed up when she'd asked about him eating there. He'd thought it was weird at the time that she was asking if he'd had lunch. Later on, he'd realized she'd asked because she'd seen him come out of Lago. Ever since then, she'd acted a little bit suspicious of him.

Kevin knew he'd screwed up and had to fix it. Luckily, he'd only said he hadn't eaten lunch, not that he hadn't been in Lago. Tonight had presented the perfect opportunity to explain further. The real truth was he had been meeting his contact in the alley behind the building. Thankfully, he really did have a cousin that worked there, so his little white lie would hold up if Jo checked it out.

But would she check it out? Kevin got the distinct impression she didn't really trust him. Why should she? He was going behind her back to feed information to his contact. Then again, the contact had alluded that Sam and Jo weren't necessarily on the right side of the law, and if they were doing something sketchy, then wasn't it Kevin's duty to report it?

Jo hadn't admitted that they were investigating Tyler's death. Kevin wasn't stupid, and if they thought they'd been able to hide their activities from him, they were wrong. It was just one of the many things they did to exclude him. Aside from tonight, they'd never made any overtures to hang around with him outside of work other than that one cookout he'd invited them to at his place.

Then again, other than the one cookout, Kevin hadn't made overtures either. And they'd gone out of their way to include him in this suicide investigation. Sam had even said he'd done good work in checking on the gun's serial number without being asked. It was the first time Kevin had done anything without being asked--maybe he should do that more.

He turned off Main Street and headed toward his house, his spirit sinking as the sun dipped below the mountains. He felt as if he were caught between a rock and a hard place. He wanted to do the right thing, but was the right thing giving information to his contact about what Sam and Jo were doing, or were Sam and Jo the ones who were doing the right thing and giving information to his contact was the wrong thing?

Kevin didn't know the answer. The best he could do was keep his eyes and ears open and collect all the information he could. Knowing what he could about everything that was going on would only benefit him in the long run. And once he knew all the information, *then* he'd be able to figure out which side he was on.

CHAPTER NINE

J o loved the little cottage she rented deep in the forest outside of town. It was set out on a back road away from everyone else. The woods teemed with wildlife--birds, chipmunks, squirrels, deer. Turkeys often pecked their way through her yard, and she could hear the owls hooting at night and the hollow echo of woodpeckers drilling the trees during the day. A few feet behind the cottage, a bubbling stream flowed over smooth rocks. The stream was only about six inches deep, but it was enough to dip her feet in so the cold mountain water could cool them on a hot summer day.

When she'd come to White Rock four years ago, she'd had no intention of staying. Even so, she'd given the cottage a homey feel, keeping the outside tidy and planting lots of flowers. Impatiens in white, coral, and red lined the perimeter of the house. Vibrant purple petunias hung from baskets, their flower-laden stems reaching almost to the ground. Colorful pansies bobbed and weaved at her from the planters that lined the porch railings.

Inside, the cottage was just as charming. She'd furnished it with flea market and thrift store finds. Overstuffed sofas and chipped white paint all in the classical muted tones that magazines referred to as cottage chic.

The cottage had the comfortable feeling of home, but it was missing something. Other living creatures. Jo wasn't one to form deep relationships. Sure, she worked closely with Sam and considered him to be one of her best friends--well, practically her only friend--but the relationship was mostly relegated to work. She didn't like getting close to anyone because she knew from bitter experience they could be ripped away without a moment's notice.

She made only one concession to that rule--her goldfish, Finn. Right now, Finn was floating around happily in his round goldfish bowl that she kept on the antique sideboard she used for a TV stand in the living room. She'd moved him from the kitchen counter a few weeks ago, figuring he might also like the company of the TV. The fish wasn't very stimulating when stacked up against human company, but he never argued with her and was easy to care for.

Jo peered inside the bowl at the golden-orange colored goldfish, and he turned toward her. Was the water getting cloudy? Maybe she should spring for the oblong fish tank with the filter that the man at the pet store had said would be better for Finn's longevity. Somehow the tank had seemed like too much of a commitment, but maybe it was time to start thinking about putting down roots here and committing. She'd gotten quite comfortable in White Rock. She liked it here. She liked the people. And she liked her job. The thoughts of moving on that had plagued her when she'd first come had subsided, and now, for the first time in her adult life, she actually thought she'd found a place where she could spend the rest of her life. After all, Sam had been born here, and he hadn't gotten tired of the area yet.

She wondered what it was like, though, to have a close family like Sam and his daughters. She wasn't close with her sister. Any advances she'd made toward helping her had been rebuked. Apparently Bridgett preferred to live in drug-addicted squalor. Should Jo have made more of an effort?

She unscrewed the cap on Finn's yellow plastic flake food container and took out a big flake. She held it just above the water on the top of the bowl.

Finn darted up, his lips piercing the top of the water and sucking the flake in as if it were one of Billie's gourmet cheeseburgers. She'd been working on hand-feeding the fish for a few weeks, and now he would come on command. It was a little thing but had created a bond between them, and Jo wondered what other tricks she could teach him. Would he roll over like Lucy?

Of course, having a fish wasn't anything like having a dog. Jo's landlord had been adamant that she not have any animals, so adopting Lucy had been out of the question, and besides, Lucy was clearly Sam's dog. She would have to make do with bonding with Lucy at work like everyone else in the office. Even Kevin had taken to the dog, much to her surprise. He'd seemed reluctant at first, almost as if he were afraid that Dupont would catch them with the dog and he would get in trouble. Tonight, Kevin had even gone out of his way to bring the special treats to her.

Perhaps she had misjudged Kevin. His explanation as to why he'd been at Lago made perfect sense. But the way he offered to help in Tyler's case had set her on edge. He must've caught on to the fact that they were investigating. She'd have to warn Sam to be more careful at work when they talked about it. She still wasn't sure it was a good idea to let anyone else know about their stealth investigatory activities.

She made her way into the bedroom, past her queen-size bed with the powder-blue silk bedspread and over to the white-painted scroll armoire. She flipped up the corner of the rose-decorated rug on which the trunk at the end of her bed sat and picked up the small silver skeleton key then fitted it into the armoire and opened the doors.

The armoire didn't contain clothing, jewelry, or any of the other things that most women kept. This one contained photographs, casework, and paperwork. It wasn't a closet. It was a workstation.

On the right side hung photographs and old papers that had to do with her sister's disappearance. Yellowed newspaper clippings. Handwritten notes she'd taken herself after researching old police files. Her heart twisted as unwanted childhood memories flooded back. Images of her sister, only a child the last time she'd seen her, laughing and smiling flickered through her mind, and then they were gone, replaced with images of her sister's toys sitting unused for over a year. Images of her mother's drawn face as she sank further into depression the longer it went with no news about her sister.

The day her sister had disappeared, Jo hadn't lost just her sister--she'd lost her mother too. Maybe that was why Jo was compelled to find out what really happened. It was like an obsession. She'd thought about asking for Sam's help a dozen times, but this one was hers alone. It was too personal. She didn't want anyone else to know she was looking. Maybe if she found the answer, she could finally stop torturing herself about what had happened to her sister. Had she suffered? Had she been terrified? And the final question... was she dead or alive?

Jo wasn't going to work on her sister's case tonight, though. She opened the left-hand side of the armoire. This one was less populated but with more recent photos. Photos of Tyler lying on the asphalt in front of his car. The inside of his police car. The car pulled over to the side of the road with a flat tire. The ashtray with the partial fingerprint. The dusting of cocaine. All of which had led nowhere.

Maybe this new lead of the large deposit into his account would give them something. She pulled her laptop out of the drawer and got to work.

CHAPTER TEN

The next day, Sam and Jo headed over to Margie Donnelly's. Sam had called ahead to make sure it was okay. Given Margie's condition, he didn't want to just barge in. Margie hadn't been surprised at the news that they'd positively identified the body. She seemed to have come to terms with the fact it was Mike. Sam guessed when you were facing a death sentence yourself, the mourning of a lost loved one took on a different meaning.

Margie had asked that they bring Lucy. Everyone in town knew about the police dog, and she was very popular. When Sam and Jo arrived, the Donnelly children were there as well. Sam had already done his homework on the family and knew that Brian Donnelly was in his early thirties and Melody in her midthirties. They were both married.

Melody met them at the door. "Chief Mason, nice of you to stop by." She juggled the stack of mail she was carrying into her left hand and held out her right. "I'm Melody Donnelly... Well, my last name's actually Marchand, but you know."

Her handshake was limp, and her eyes were red rimmed from crying.

"I'm sorry about your loss, ma'am. This is Sergeant Jody Harris."

Melody nodded to Jo and ushered them in. She turned to a man that was seated in the living room. "This is my brother, Brian."

They exchanged greetings as Melody put the stack of bills down on the table. Sam's eyes followed it. "I've been taking care of Mom's things for her. She can't handle this anymore, and Dad wasn't any good at it." Melody's voice caught, and Sam gave her a moment to compose herself. "Cancer's expensive, and these bills need to be handled."

Sam's eyes stayed on the bills. Cancer was expensive. And he knew that even if you had good insurance, it didn't always cover everything. Would Mike's life insurance help the family out?

Lucy trotted into the dining room and went straight to Margie, who was seated at the table. She looked even worse than she had the day before. Laid out in front of her was a pile of silver and the flow blue china Sam had seen in the cabinet. Margie's face brightened at the sight of Lucy, and she bent down with effort to pat the dog. Lucy licked her, sniffed the edge of the table, then moved on to the walker that sat beside Margie, apparently finding something interesting to sniff on the bottom. Sam's heart pinched. Margie hadn't had to use a walker when they'd visited the day before. Was she really failing that fast, or had Mike's death hastened it?

"I'm just putting things in order," Margie said. "Don't want to leave the kids with a mess now."

"Listen, Chief," Brian said. "We'd like to make arrangements for my father. We were wondering... about the body."

"Well, that's the thing," Sam said. "We'd like to do a few more tests."

Melody frowned. "Tests? Why would you need to test anything? He shot himself."

"He was shot, yes."

"You mean you think someone else shot him?" Margie asked. "Who the hell would do that?"

"That's what I was gonna ask you. Had Mike tried to kill himself before? Did he have any enemies?"

Brian shot up from his chair. "Of course he never tried to kill himself! And everyone liked him." He gestured toward his mother. "You could see why he would be upset. Haven't we been through enough?

Are you going to drag this out now and cause my mother further suffering?"

"We're not going to drag it out. That's the last thing we want," Sam said. "But we have a certain protocol, and certain criteria must be satisfied before we can rule his death a suicide."

Margie struggled to get up from the table. She clutched the walker, her bony knuckles turning white with the effort to help herself stand.

"You don't have to get up, ma'am," Sam said.

"I need to while I still can. I'm getting a lot worse, but I'm not dead yet. And if something happened to Mike, I want to find out what it was. But like I told you, he was very depressed, and I don't know of anyone that would want to kill him."

"Did he argue or fight with anyone recently?" Sam asked.

Margie snorted. "Just that Lucas Thorne."

Sam's left brow shot up. "They had a fight? What did they fight about?"

"He came sniffing around about selling the land again. Probably heard I was sick and wanted to take advantage."

"He was always asking about that." Brian pointed to the bills on the table. "Maybe Dad should have been thinking about selling, but it's ludicrous to think someone like Thorne would kill my father over the land."

"Probably. But we need to consider every angle," Sam said.

Brian crossed his arms over his chest. "Seems like a waste of taxpayer money."

Sam nodded. "I just want to cover all the bases. I'm sure the medical examiner will be done with his full investigation any day, and we'll be able to clear this all up. I don't want to put you people through any more than you're already going through." He turned to Margie. "Mike wasn't thinking of selling to Thorne, was he?"

Margie leaned on her walker. Her body was frail, but her voice was strong. "No way. He told that bastard that he'd get the farm over his dead body and then sent him packing."

CHAPTER ELEVEN

"So what do you think?" Sam asked once he and Jo were in the Tahoe heading back to the police station.

"Hard to say. I realize the family is upset with everything going on, but it seemed to me that the son protested a little too much at us continuing the investigation," Jo said.

Lucy whined from her place in the backseat as if in agreement.

Sam looks at Jo out of the corner of his eye. "Did you get a chance to look into that deposit and Tyler's account?"

"I had to call in a few favors. Since we can't get a subpoena for that information, it has to be done in a different way," Jo said. "I happen to know a few people, and we should have some information soon."

Sometimes it was hard being a cop--everything you did was tracked and recorded. Maybe that wasn't always the best way to serve justice. But with the strange things coming up in Tyler's case, Sam wasn't exactly sure if serving justice was going to end up the way he'd previously thought it would.

Reese was waiting for them anxiously inside the lobby of the police station. The way her sneaker-clad foot was tapping out a rhythm on the marble floor indicated to Sam that she had some interesting news.

Lucy ran straight over to Reese's desk and sniffed at the drawer. Reese opened it and fed her a treat.

"I think we might want to lay off the treats," Sam said. "We don't want her getting fat. I'm feeding her a premium dog food at home. These snacks might not be good for her."

"Kevin brought them in special," Reese said. "We don't give them to her a lot."

"Where is Kevin?" Jo peeked over the post office box divider. "He's not in there."

"He clocked out already," Reese said. "I have good news and bad news."

"Bad news first?" Sam phrased it as a question. He wasn't sure which he wanted first.

"The glasses were washed. Only Mike's fingerprints and some touch DNA that was a partial match."

"That was quick." *And inconclusive,* Sam thought. Having a partial match meant anyone from Mike's family could have left the DNA, but everyone knew the family used the camp, so there was nothing new there. Even though the drinking glasses were clearly used that night, Sam knew it didn't prove a thing.

"I have friends in high places," Reese said.

"Okay, so what's the good news?" Jo asked.

"John sent this over from the autopsy." She held up a piece of paper and wiggled it in the air.

"What's it say?" Sam asked. Judging by the look on Reese's face, he knew it was something interesting.

Reese handed it over, and Sam looked at it while Reese gave him the abridged version of the technical report.

"There wasn't enough of the fingers left to test for gunshot powder. Mike was right-handed, and that's the hand that the birds worked on the most. He got the partial print from the other hand." Reese grimaced. "Anyway, judging by the trajectory of the bullet, the placement of the gun, and the lack of gunshot powder, John thinks we need more investigation before we rule it a suicide."

An undercurrent of electricity ran through Sam.

His gut feeling had been right. Could someone have killed Mike? He looked down at the report. Time of death was fixed at between six fifty and seven twenty that night. "Says here he died around seven p.m."

"At least gives us something to go on." Jo headed toward the K-Cup machine, grabbing her bright-yellow smiley mug and shoving it under the spout. "First order of business, find out where our favorite suspects were around seven p.m."

"The only people that could get into the logging road are people that have the key for that gate. That being Mike's family and the others that have camps up that road." Sam wondered if Thorne could've gotten the gate key somehow. He had contacts and knew people in high--and low--places. Sam wouldn't put it past him to have bribed someone at the logging company to give him keys to all the logging roads for his nefarious drug-dealing activities. The mountain trails in there would be perfect for trans-porting all over the county.

"Only the Ritchies have a cabin on Logging Road Number Four. The rest of the land is empty," Reese said.

Jo pulled her mug out from under the spout of the machine then turned to look at Sam over her shoulder. "Coffee?"

"Yeah. Thanks. Looks like we need to go interview the neighbors and back to the family again. They could have a motive if Mike's life insurance was going to pay out. Margie had a lot of medical bills, and Mike wouldn't sell the farm to pay for them. Maybe the kids didn't want to get dragged down by that. Guess we better make these coffees to go."

"Not so fast, Chief," Reese said and then at Sam's confused look added, "Remember how you asked me to call in some of those candidates for the job opening?"

"Uh-huh." Sam had forgotten.

Reese thrust her chin toward the front door. "Well, one of them is coming in for his interview right now."

CHAPTER TWELVE

Sam spent an hour interviewing Gary Newport. He sat him in the chair with the shorter leg that they normally put suspects in to throw them off balance. Sam thought it might work just as well for seeing how job applicants reacted to having the added stress of a wobbly chair.

Gary, who was in his midthirties, seemed competent enough. He had the right things on his resume, but Sam just couldn't get excited about him. He needed more than some bullet points on a resume and a good education. He needed to get a feeling about the person. But with Dupont on his case about filling the job, Sam didn't have all summer to wait for the perfect candidate. Maybe the perfect one would never come along.

After the interview, Sam grabbed a ring of keys

out of his middle drawer. He'd almost forgotten that he'd been given the keys to the logging roads when he'd taken the job. He'd never had to use them before, and he really didn't need to use them now either because Reese had called the Ritchies to let them know they were on their way, and they'd opened the gate for him. He brought them along just in case.

The Ritchies' camp was just like the Donnellys', cobbled together with bits and pieces. It was nothing fancy, but it served its purpose. Nancy put out coffee, and they all sat around the kitchen table as if it were a social visit.

"So what is it you want to know, Chief?" Nancy asked. "Surely you're not going to arrest Bullwinkle."

Sam smiled. "Bullwinkle had nothing to do with it. Mike was shot. Bullwinkle must've been spooked by something, and that's why he ran by your place so fast."

Nancy's hand flew up to her heart, and her mouth gaped open. "Shot? By whom?"

"That's what we need to find out." Jo leaned her elbows on the table. "Have you seen anyone at the camp? Maybe a car that didn't belong?"

Bill shook his head. "Only ever saw one of the Donnellys' cars here. The truck and the brown Ford.

The kids didn't bother with the camp too much, so it was mostly Mike's truck."

Nancy pressed her lips together. "Of course, our camp is beyond theirs, so anyone visiting their camp wouldn't have driven by here. We try to bring all our supplies in so we don't have to go into town, and we don't leave much once we get here. So it's possible another car was there. We wouldn't have seen it."

"Did you hear anything unusual that night? Gunshots or yelling?" Sam asked.

Nancy shook her head. "No... Oh wait! That was the night we heard those darn ATVs. It used to be so quiet up here. That's what we loved about it, but lately there's been kids on those ATVs, and in the winter, the snowmobile noise makes quite a ruckus."

Bill nodded his head in agreement. "That's why we didn't hear the gunshot. Those kids aren't just joyriding on ATVs. I think they're out poaching deer and God knows what else."

Sam frowned. In his book, poaching was as big a crime as murder. Hunting seasons were in place so that the population of wildlife remained healthy. He hated it when people ignored that. "So you did hear gunshots?"

"Rifles. Is that what Mike was shot with?"

Sam shook his head. "No, but with all that noise going on, you probably wouldn't notice another gun.

Do you think the ATVs were at the Donnelly property?"

Nancy shrugged. "Hard to tell. The noise did come from that direction, but if you want to know for sure, why don't you ask that Jesse Cowly? He's one of the kids that rides on them."

"Jesse Cowly? Are you sure?" Jo shot a look at Sam. Jesse Cowly was a local that flirted with the wrong side of the law. Sam had caught him in minor crimes but had always let him go, thinking it might not be a bad idea if Jesse owed him.

Thing was, Sam had a suspicion that Jesse was involved in Thorne's drug ring. And if Jesse and his friends were involved with Thorne and the ATVs were over at Mike Donnelly's, maybe his theory that Thorne had killed Mike to get his farmland wasn't so far-fetched.

ON THE WAY out from the neighbors', Sam and Jo stopped at the Donnellys' to look for the ATV tracks. Sam didn't recall any tracks being there before the pictures, and he was pretty good at remembering the specifics of a crime scene, but it never hurt to take a second look.

"Did you see any ATV tracks in the grass when

we found Mike's body? The tracks in the grass probably wouldn't be there anymore," Jo said as they let Lucy out of the back of the SUV.

"I don't think so," Sam said. "But Kevin's pictures would probably tell us if there were."

They went around to the side. The grass was still stained a muddy red. Lucy sniffed around but apparently didn't find anything of interest and trotted off toward the driveway.

They stood looking out at the woods, where birds chirped and flew from branch to branch. A tufted titmouse swooped down to the ground. A chipmunk poked its head out of a decaying woodpile.

It was quiet out there. No signs of ATVs now. Just the rustle of leaves and the slight summer breeze. "I don't know if there are many trails in this area for all-terrain vehicles." Sam walked over to the edge of the woods. It was midafternoon, and the low sun elongated the shadows of the tree trunks. He could see a thin deer path but nothing that was wide enough for an ATV.

"Maybe they drove right up the road," Jo said.

They slowly crossed the front yard to the driveway.

"So what did you think of the guy you interviewed?" she asked.

Sam shrugged. "He was okay. I might like to get your take on some of these interviewees."

Jo made a face, and Sam laughed. "I know it's a pain in the ass. But we have to hire someone, and it'll be a lot more pleasant for us if it's someone we like."

"Sure, I get that." Jo stopped at the edge of the driveway, where Lucy was sniffing the tire tracks. The driveway was dirt and a little bit muddy. It had rained two days earlier, and the sun didn't hit the driveway directly, so the dirt stayed damp for a long time. Mike Donnelly's truck was still in the driveway. She could see the tire tracks leading up to it. But there were other tire marks.

"These are Mike's tracks, but looks like there was another car here recently, too," Jo pointed out.

"The Ritchies said they saw the other family car here. Maybe one of the kids or Margie came out," Sam said.

Lucy was sniffing at something on the edge of the driveway. She barked then looked at Jo and Sam.

"What have you got?" Jo squatted next to Lucy.

"What do you think this is?" She looked up at Sam. "A bicycle track?"

Sam looked at the thin track. It was barely even noticeable, but he could faintly see several tracks as if the bike had been ridden back and forth. "Sure looks like it. It's certainly not from any ATV. Those tires would be wider than this but not as wide as the car."

Jo stood. "A lot of people ride their bikes out here. There's even a bike trail in the woods."

"And the Donnellys have bikes up on the porch."

"So it's not much of a lead." Jo pulled open the passenger door of the Tahoe and let Lucy jump in before getting in herself. Sam was still in the driveway, and she leaned across the car and talked to him through the open driver's window. "We need to find those ATV riders and ask them exactly where they were riding. They might have seen something, though chances are slim they'll admit to being here if they were poaching deer."

Sam opened his door and got into the driver's seat. "Even slimmer if they were involved in the murder."

CHAPTER THIRTEEN

J esse Cowly lived in an old run-down 1950s ranch with one of his buddies. Jo and Sam knew it was a party house, and after swinging by the auto-body shop where he worked and discovering it was Jesse's day off, they decided to pay a visit to him at home. It was late afternoon, so Jesse and his roommate would be up and probably doing something illegal.

The house was painted a faded blue. Faded black shutters hung on the windows. The front yard consisted of brown patches of dirt and weeds. A section of screen flapped down from the top corner of the screen door. A dirty curtain flapped in and out of one of the open windows in tempo to the loud music blaring from inside.

Jo pulled the brim of her cap down and secured

her sunglasses. She figured that made her look more official and a little bit more badass.

Sam knocked on the door. Loudly.

The music volume was lowered, and the door opened to reveal Jesse's bleary-eyed, puffy face. He looked at Sam, and his eyes widened then darted to Jo. "Uhhh... Can I help you guys?"

"Yeah. We got some questions." Sam pushed his way into the house. He didn't act confrontational, but Jesse got the message.

Jesse stumbled back a little bit. "Hey, you can't just come in here, can you?"

"Sure we can. We're the police," Sam said.

Lucy pushed her way in beside Sam and stood at attention, her eyes trained on Jesse. Jesse's gaze flicked to Lucy with alarm.

Jesse's roommate, Brian Carlson, bolted up from the couch, sweeping something that had been sitting on the coffee table next to a crusty pizza box under the couch. The house was spiced with the sweet smell of pot mixed with stale beer and greasy pepperoni. A cloud of smoke hung over Brian's head, and he waved it away.

"This is entrapment or something, isn't it?" Jesse's eyes darted around the room as if he was looking for other things he should hide.

"Calm down." Jo pushed Jesse into a chair. "We're

not here to arrest you for anything you might be doing in here." She looked around the room pointedly.

Lucy sat in front of Jesse's chair and stared at him.

"We have some questions about your ATV activity out down near the logging roads," Sam said.

Jesse and Brian exchanged a look. "What do you mean?"

"Nancy Ritchie said you guys ride around back there in the woods." Jo lifted the top of the pizza box carefully with her index finger. Inside was congealed cheesy pizza. She let the lid flop back down.

"No, she must be mistaken." Jesse leaned back in his chair. Apparently he was trying to look relaxed, but it just made him look more nervous.

Lucy let out a low growl, and his gaze flicked to her.

Jo decided to capitalize on Jesse's nervousness by making her way around the room and looking into various boxes and behind sofas while Sam asked them questions about where they were the night Mike had died. She even picked up the corner of the rug.

"Hey, you can't search in here like that," Brian said.

Lucy swiveled her head in his direction and barked.

"We can if we have probable cause like a witness telling us you were out on those roads," Sam lied. "Our witness also heard gunshots out there. What do you know about that?"

The two looked at each other. Brian said, "We don't know anything about any gunshots, right?"

"I might ride an ATV once in a while, but I don't know anything about any gunshots," Jesse said.

"Really? Where were you Monday night?" Sam asked.

"We were right here." Jesse's answer tumbled out way too fast.

Lucy inched closer to Jesse and growled.

Jo could see that Jesse and Brian would try to deny they had been there, but she knew how to make them tell the truth. Her experience with most small-time criminals like Jesse proved that they would easily confess to something minor if they thought they were going to be nailed for a bigger crime.

"Really?" She came to stand in the center of the room. "That's funny because we know someone who says otherwise. This person saw you out there right about the time that Mike Donnelly was shot."

The looks of surprise on their faces were almost

comical. Apparently, they hadn't known about the shooting. Jo wasn't surprised, though--she didn't think Jesse was the type to escalate his criminal activities to murder. But she did think he had something to do with Thorne's drug operation, and she knew Sam had let him off on a few minor things. She figured Sam was grooming him to be an informant, looking the other way on lesser crimes so that Jesse owed him and he could use him later to catch the big fish.

"We don't know anything about Mike Donnelly." Brian's face had turned white.

"Really?" Sam leaned against the wall and crossed his arms over his chest. "Well then, how do you explain being seen out there at the time he died?"

"And why would you lie about it, if you weren't involved?" Jo asked.

Jesse held his hands up. "Okay, okay. We were out there, but we didn't kill anybody. We were just joyriding on our ATVs."

"You expect us to believe that? We've got DNA evidence from the body just waiting at the lab, and my bet is that it has your signature all over it, and even if it doesn't, we've got witnesses, and they saw you with guns." Sam smiled. "Oh, did I mention that Mike was shot? I wonder if we'll find the same kind of gun in here."

"What? No way! We didn't shoot anyone." Jesse shifted in his chair. Lucy edged closer. A bead of sweat formed on Jesse's forehead.

"Well then, explain to me why you were out there with a gun," Sam said.

"Screw it," Jesse said. "I'd rather get in trouble for poaching than murder. We were out there poaching deer. We don't know anything about Mike Donnelly getting shot."

Sam appeared to think it over, causing Jesse and Brian to become even more nervous. "But you *were* out there near the Donnelly cabin?"

Jesse shook his head. "Not near it. But we rode up the logging road past it to access the trails in the back."

"I told you we should have started at the trail on the other side of the woods," Brian muttered.

"If you rode up the road, then you would've gone past the Donnellys' place," Jo said. "Do you know what time that was?"

"Shortly before sunset," Jesse said. He looked at Brian then shrugged. "The deer come out at dusk, and we wanted to be in place in the field by then."

It was June, and the sun set around seven. If someone had been at Mike's, Jesse and Brian might've seen them. "When you drove by, did you see anyone at the Donnellys' camp or anything strange going on there?"

Jesse screwed up his face and thought for a second. "I didn't see anything funny going on, just a couple cars in the driveway."

"A *couple* of cars?" Sam said. "What did they look like?"

"One was a big black truck. I've seen that one in the driveway before, but the other one was a small white car, a VW Jetta. I recognized it because my sister drives one," Jesse said.

"Do you know who was driving that Jetta?" Sam asked.

Jesse shook his head and shrugged. "No, man. Sorry. But whoever it was must have been in the cabin, because I know there was no one outside."

CHAPTER FOURTEEN

The Ritchies had said that only the family cars had been in the driveway, so Sam and Jo headed off to the Donnellys' to find out who drove a white Jetta and deliver the news that Mike's death might not have been by his own hand. Since Margie had seemed to be fond of Lucy, they brought her again. Melody answered their knock, her eyes narrowing when she saw them.

"I hope you're here to tell us you're releasing Dad's body." Melody stood in the door, giving the distinct impression she wasn't going to invite them in.

"Can we come in?" Sam asked gently.

Melody's eyes flicked to Lucy and then back up to Sam. "Okay, but just because Mom likes the dog. She's not feeling good today."

Margie was lying on the couch, a colorful afghan wrapped around her. Brian sat in the chair. He tensed when he saw Sam and Jo. Lucy trotted over to Margie, and Margie's eyes flickered open. She put her hand out to stroke Lucy's fur, a ghost of a smile passing over her lips.

"Sorry to interrupt, ma'am," Sam said.

Brian pushed up from his chair and crossed his arms over his chest. "I hope you're gonna let us bury my father while my mom can still make it to the funeral."

"We'll be releasing the body today." Sam paused and cleared his throat. "But I'm afraid the medical examiner wasn't able to specifically rule that your father shot himself."

Melody's brows knitted together. "What are you talking about?"

Margie struggled to sit up on the couch. Lucy sat at her feet, Margie's hand still rubbing the dog's head. "What's he saying, Melly?"

Sam walked over to stand in front of Margie. "Mike might not have shot himself."

"What do you mean? He's not dead?"

"He is. But someone else might have killed him."

"Oh, but he was so depressed. I just thought..." Margie's face crinkled, and she looked up at Sam. "Who would do such a thing?"

"Someone who was angry with him or benefitted from his death."

Brian scrubbed his hands across his face. "What? Nobody would *benefit* from his death. He barely had any life insurance. And no one would want my father dead. Everybody liked him. You guys must be wrong."

"I don't think we are," Sam said.

Melody collapsed into a chair. "I don't believe it. I thought he was shot with his own gun."

"He was. Which makes me think he might've been expecting an argument with someone. Otherwise, why would he have taken his gun from the house and brought it to the camp? He didn't normally do that, did he?"

"No. He would bring the rifles at hunting season but not the revolver," Margie said.

"He could've been expecting a fight or some kind of altercation," Jo suggested. "Is there anyone you can think of?"

"Nobody except Thorne." Margie's hands stilled on Lucy's head, and her gaze jerked up to Sam. "But you don't think he would..."

"Hard telling," Sam said.

"We know Mike was at the cabin that night. His truck is still there. But which one of you drives the white Jetta?"

They all looked at each other.

"My car is a red Toyota," Melody said. "And Mom drives a brown Ford Taurus."

"I have a truck like Dad's." Brian looked down at the floor, and Sam glanced at Jo. Was he not telling them everything?

"Were you all here at the house that night?" Sam asked.

Margie smiled wryly. "I don't get out much anymore."

Jo sat next to Margie on the couch and patted her hand.

Sam looked at Brian and Melody. "And you two were here with her? Did you go to the cabin with your dad that day at all?"

"This is all so tiring." Margie looked drained, as if this news was sucking what life was left out of her. Sam's heart clenched. It was messy business, but he owed it to Mike Donnelly to get to the bottom of it. Especially if Thorne was involved.

Melody went to her mother, protectively tucking in the afghan and shooting angry looks at Sam and Jo.

"I think my mother has had quite enough now." She ushered them out of the room toward the foyer. "Mom's declining rapidly. Just the other day, she was driving, and today, she can barely walk around the house. The doctor said that would happen after she stopped chemo and the cancer started to grow rapidly. I don't know if all this business about my father is good for her. Can't you people go easy on her?"

"We'll try to bother her as little as possible. Maybe you can help us with just one thing. We need to create a timeline, and I was wondering if any of you could remember what your father did that day. Who he talked to. Did either of you see him or talk to him? Did he mention anything? Did he sound off at all?" Sam asked.

"I talked to him that morning on the phone, and he sounded fine," Brian said.

"I saw him at lunch, and he seemed fine, too," Melody said.

"And where were you both that night?" Sam asked.

Brian looked at his shoes. "I've been having some car trouble. But that night I was at home."

"Where do you live?" Jo asked. "Is there anyone else who could verify?"

"I can," Melody said. At Brian's funny look, she continued. "I wasn't there, but I was picking up Mom's pills at the pharmacy across the street. You can see into Brian's apartment, and I always look over to see if he's home. I was waving like a crazy person out on the sidewalk to catch his attention, but I guess he didn't see me."

"No. I didn't see you over there. I don't look out the window all the time."

"Of course not. But I saw you. I didn't have time to go over and visit because Mom needed her pills right away. She'd almost run out, and I didn't want her to be in pain."

"What time was that?" Jo asked.

Melody pressed her lips together. "I'd say it was around seven p.m. I'd gotten out of work at the flower shop late and picked up some fast food. Joel-- that's my husband--was working at the hospital. He's an RN. Mom needed the pills, and Dad wasn't around. I had no idea that he'd be..."

"Do either of you know anyone that has a white Jetta? A family member or friend of your Dad's?" Sam asked.

Brian and Melody looked at each other and shook their heads.

"Why are you here asking *us* this stuff? Why aren't you out there finding Dad's killer?" Brian asked. "*We* sure didn't kill him."

"That's exactly what we're doing. Starting here with the people that knew him the best. We figure you would know what was going on with him, and that could help us find who did this," Jo said.

"Well, we don't know anything," Melody said. "Mom and Dad didn't have a lot. Just this run-down farm, and the life insurance is minimal. Won't even cover Mom's co-pays on her medical bills. And everyone liked my father. Like Mom said, about the only person he ever fought with was Thorne."

CHAPTER FIFTEEN

S am dropped Jo off at the station to double-check on the value of Mike's life insurance. He sent Lucy in with her. He had an idea of where to look for the white Jetta, and he didn't want the dog to get hurt.

He headed up Prickett Hill to the site of the condo village that Thorne was building. Once beautiful woods with a view of the lakes below, it was now clear cut, a scar on the landscape that made Sam's stomach tighten with disgust.

The site was still under construction, and Thorne had a plush office inside the construction trailer that Sam had been inside only once before. The opulence had surprised him. Every other construction trailer he'd been inside of had been utilitarian and plain, but Thorne's was done up like the inside of a Las Vegas suite.

Before Sam knocked on the door, he made an inspection of the parking lot. There was no white Jetta. But, then again, if Thorne had people that worked for him doing his dirty work, they probably didn't also work at the construction site. He probably kept them far away from his legitimate business.

Sam looped back around. The sound of machinery grinding, men yelling, and metal beams clanging rang in his ears. Thorne's red Cadillac was parked beside the trailer on the side that was away from the construction. Thorne must park it there on purpose so it wouldn't be marred by a stray nail or get dirt on it.

Sam knocked on the thin metal door.

"Come in."

Sam opened the door and stepped in.

Thorne was seated at a mahogany desk. He looked tan and healthy in his button-down shirt, but when you looked closely, you could see the signs of aging in his dyed-black hair and slightly thickening middle. The surface of the desk was stacked neatly with folders and paperwork. A gold penholder sat on the edge.

He looked up, an immediate scowl crossing his brow. "What are you doing here?"

"Police business," Sam said.

Thorne stood but stayed behind the desk, keeping the piece of furniture between them. "We have our permits, and there's been no police calls, so..." Thorne spread his hands, adopting his usual cocky manner.

"I'm not here about permits. I'm here about Mike Donnelly."

"I heard about his suicide. What's that got to do with me?" Did Thorne's lips quirk up in a slight smile, or was Sam imagining it?

"Yeah, turns out it wasn't a suicide." Sam stepped a little closer to the desk. "And in tracking down suspects, we discovered that you had a beef going with Mike."

"I wouldn't necessarily call it a beef. I offered to buy his land. I was doing them a favor. They were getting older, and the farm is in disrepair. They couldn't handle it anymore," Thorne said.

"I don't think Mike saw it as a favor, though, did he?"

"He wasn't ready to sell yet," Thorne said. "But I figured he'd come around soon, especially with his wife and all those medical bills."

"So you went to his cabin to try to persuade him, and when that didn't work, you shot him," Sam said.

Thorne laughed. "Shot him for land? I didn't have

to resort to that. All I had to do was wait him out. Those kids were chomping at the bit to sell."

A seed of unease sprouted in Sam's gut. If what Brian had said about Mike's life insurance was true, they wouldn't get anything from his life insurance, but they sure would get a bundle from the sale of the farm. "But they wouldn't be able to do that until they inherited the land. And even though Margie didn't have long, Mike had been fit as a fiddle."

"Maybe so, but once a man's wife dies, his priorities change. Kids often have more influence."

"Maybe you didn't want to wait for the kids to influence him. Maybe you took matters into your own hands, knowing that Margie was going to die soon and Mike was the only thing standing in your way."

"Are you accusing me of murder, Chief?" Thorne asked.

Sam leaned over the desk and got right in his face. "Where were you at seven p.m. two nights ago?"

Thorne narrowed his eyes and stepped around the desk, so close to Sam that he could smell his spicy aftershave. The move surprised Sam. Usually, Thorne was weaselly, not confrontational. He preferred to do things behind your back. But the move told Sam that Thorne was confident. Why was that?

"Listen, Chief Mason. You can go around accusing me all you want. I'm not afraid, because I didn't kill Mike, so you can't prove that I did. But if I were you, I would think twice about continuing to accuse me, because turnabout's fair play, and if you run around town accusing me of killing someone, then I might just have to do the same for you."

"What are you talking about?"

"Don't think I don't know what happened twenty years ago. I'm in tight with Harley Dupont, and Dupont has connections. Connections that might even have solid proof about your extracurricular activities back then." Thorne smirked, turned, and walked back behind his desk. He waved a dismissive hand at Sam. "So if I were you, I would go about my business and look for the real killer before casting accusations and getting yourself into a heap of trouble you won't be able to get out of."

CHAPTER SIXTEEN

When Sam got back to the station, Jo and Reese were feeding Lucy pot roast from the diner. It was near quitting time, and the homey smell of dinner made Sam's stomach growl. He didn't have anyone at home to cook for him. His daughters had left the day before, and the fridge was bare. Looked like he'd be eating dinner at Holy Spirits.

Sam headed straight for the coffee machine. The meeting with Thorne had rattled him. How much did Thorne know about what had happened twenty years ago? How could he know anything?

Thorne was probably just bluffing. How could Dupont know anything? He'd barely known Gracie, as far as Sam could tell. Mick was back from his trip, and the threat involved Mick as well, and maybe he could shed some light on it. Sam took out his cell phone and thumbed in a text to Mick to meet him at Holy Spirits.

"There's over three hundred white Jettas in the county," said Kevin, who was seated at his desk watching Lucy chow down. "We need something more to go on. Like a license plate or some distinguishing mark. Being shorthanded like we are, we don't have the manpower to run down all these cars in a timely manner."

Sam grimaced. Mike's investigation had taken his focus away from interviewing people to replace Tyler, but he was starting to realize the sooner they got someone in, the better off they would be. Sam couldn't let his personal feelings about "replacing" Tyler get in the way if being shorthanded impeded their investigations.

"I called Jesse to see if he got the license plate." Jo shrugged. "It was a long shot, but I figured I'd try. He didn't, though. He barely even remembered seeing the car."

"I checked out Thorne's construction site. No white Jetta there. I figured that was a long shot too, but what the heck," Sam said.

Kevin looked up at him. "You think someone that works for Thorne is the killer?"

"Not really," Sam lied. He hadn't let Kevin in on much of the investigation Sam and Jo had done on the side regarding Thorne. Kevin had been stepping it up lately, but he just hadn't done enough yet to earn that level of trust. "Just checking every angle. Thorne had an interest in Mike's land, so I had to check it out."

"Oh yeah. Makes sense," Kevin said.

"We need to figure out another way to find out who was with Mike at the cabin. We need to start retracing what he did that day," Jo said.

Sam sipped his coffee and glanced out the window, the brew turning bitter in his mouth as he saw Mayor Dupont coming up the walkway. "Here comes trouble."

Jo and Kevin looked, each of them making a face.

"It's quitting time. I gotta run, or I'll be late for class." Reese pushed up from her chair and grabbed her slouchy hobo purse. "See you guys tomorrow."

"I better head out to Rita Hoelscher's. Nettie Deardorff got a chicken, and she claims it pecked a hole in her fence." Rita Hoelscher and Nettie Deardorff had a long-standing feud that had gone on so long that no one even remembered what started it. Kevin gave Lucy a quick pat on the head and followed Reese out, giving a curt nod to Dupont as they passed in the doorway.

Jo hastily picked up the spoils of Lucy's supper and scurried over to her desk. She usually avoided talking to Dupont because whenever she did talk to him, things slipped out of her mouth that weren't good for her career.

Dupont stopped in front of Lucy and tentatively stretched his hand out. Lucy sniffed. He petted her on the head. "Good girl."

Lucy gave Sam a look as if saying, "Do I have to be nice to him?"

Dupont's change of tune toward the dog was suspicious. Barely a month ago when they'd discovered Lucy at a crime scene, Dupont had been angry to find the dog in the station. He'd ordered them to get rid of her. They'd taken her to the animal shelter. No one had claimed her, and when she kept running away, it made her unattractive for adoption. Sam had considered adopting her, but since he spent most of his time chasing down criminals, he didn't think it would be fair to the dog.

Reese had saved the day by pulling in some favors to secure a K-9 grant for the station, and they'd been able to officially keep her. When Dupont had discovered how much the townspeople loved Lucy, he'd taken all the credit for her being on the police force.

Lucy still seemed wary of him. Sam figured she was a good judge of character.

"I know you're investigating a murder, *Chief*."

Dupont put emphasis on the last word, making it sound like an insult. "But I don't think harassing prominent residents is part of that."

Sam raised a brow. "You mean Thorne? I was just going by procedure."

Dupont's eyes narrowed. "Surely you don't suspect Lucas Thorne. He's a valuable member of our society. He brings jobs to the area and new tourists as well. All of that is good for our economy."

"Oh, is that how you justify it?" Sam asked.

Dupont's eyes flicked to Jo and then back to Sam. Jo was sitting at her desk, her pencil tapping on a pile of papers she was pretending to study while making it look as if she weren't eavesdropping.

"What are you talking about?" Dupont asked.

"All these rezoning laws that always seem to turn in Thorne's favor even though plenty of the towns-people don't want the deforestation to keep happening. If I didn't know better, I'd think you and Thorne had some kind of a deal going."

"How dare you! I am just being a good mayor and trying to help the town."

Sam crossed his arms over his chest. "Really? In some of those meetings, it seems like the town's asking for no more commercial building, but then the rezoning happens anyway. I wouldn't want anyone to look into those meeting minutes too thoroughly--they might get the wrong idea about you."

"Look into them too thoroughly?" Dupont's smarmy smile faltered as if he were just realizing maybe he could get caught at whatever it was he was doing. "What do you mean?"

"There are a lot of environmentalists that don't like what's happening here. If someone goes over the minutes, what the townspeople are saying is all in there. They might wonder why the mayor is allowing all this farmland to be moved into commercial zoning, that's all." Sam said it as if he were doing Dupont a favor by enlightening him.

"Well, I don't see how that's a problem..."

"And then if they looked back and discovered you had some kind of relationship with Thorne..." Sam shrugged. "Well, I'm sure there's nothing like that going on. Especially not with all those expensive commercials you have going. You must be busy with that, and you wouldn't have time to be involved in Thorne's business."

Dupont patted Lucy's head absently. Sam could practically see the wheels inside his head spinning. Dupont didn't need to say anything--the look on his face told Sam everything. But he'd already known Dupont was in Thorne's pocket. Thorne had probably given him money for the commercials, and Dupont had been too stupid and excited about the money to even check if those payments could be tracked. If Thorne was smart, he'd probably left a trail so he could hold it over Dupont's head.

"I don't think anyone would check on anything like that." Dupont straightened and glanced back at Jo. "And, besides, I'm not doing anything wrong."

"Well, that's good to hear, Mayor Dupont. Then you have nothing to worry about, right?" Sam asked.

"Right. Nothing to worry about." Dupont started toward the door and then turned back to Sam. "Just stay away from Thorne. Unless you have solid proof or evidence to accuse him of something, he can make your life miserable."

JO LOOKED out the window and watched Dupont walk back toward the town offices then spun around to look at Sam.

"What was that all about?" Jo asked.

"I might've pressed on Thorne a little hard. But I think he could have something to do with Mike's death." Sam glanced out the window. "Dupont's little visit pretty much proves what we suspected all along. Dupont is in Thorne's pocket."

"You don't really think Thorne is a killer, do you?

I mean, he might be behind the killing, but he's smarter than he looks. If he is involved, he's probably arranged it so that the evidence can't be linked to him."

"Probably, but we're still gonna follow it, anyway."

"Speaking of evidence, I got one of my contacts back in Boston to check on Tyler's bank account." Jo tapped the eraser end of her pencil on the pad on the desk in front of her. "Twenty thousand dollars was deposited in there the week before he died."

Sam frowned. "*Twenty thousand?*"

Jo nodded.

Sam let out a low whistle. "That's a lot of money." He paced around the squad room, running his fingers through his hair. Lucy sensed his agitation and trotted behind him. He bent down and scratched her behind the ears. "Do you think he was on the take?"

Jo pushed up from her chair and paced in the other direction. She didn't want to think that. She'd trusted Tyler. "I didn't see any signs of that. Though he was acting a little secretive the last month or so, but I mean, we *knew* Tyler. He was a good guy."

"Do you ever really know someone?" Sam asked.

Jo turned and looked at him. Even though they worked together and trusted each other and she considered them to be close friends, she didn't really *know* Sam. Not the deep-down-inside Sam. Sure, she knew a lot of things about him. Like that he'd been married twice and neither of the marriages had ended well. And that he loved his daughters more than anything. And he loved White Rock and hated the way it was being built up.

But she didn't really know what was going on inside Sam. Sometimes she sensed a deep, sad loneliness that made her want to reach out and connect with him on a deeper level. Other times she sensed a dark secret that she might be better off not knowing about.

Then again, Jo had her own secrets, and she wasn't exactly batting a thousand in the relationship department herself.

"Maybe not," she said cautiously.

"I suppose there's a lot of reasons why Tyler might've had that deposit. Maybe he had a retirement account or something and cashed it in for Clarissa's treatment."

Knowing Tyler's self-sacrificing nature, Jo wouldn't have been surprised if he cashed in on his retirement income to help. "Maybe. I can have my contact check into that."

"If only we could find out what that key goes to, we might get some answers."

"I'm beginning to wonder if we want them," Jo said.

Sam pressed his lips together. "We might not like what we find."

"But I suppose we have to find it." Jo sighed. "We might need to widen the search area. If Tyler was trying to hide something, he could have driven miles away to open a safety deposit box, post office box, or whatever to hide it in."

"Right. Not a lot of time to get into that right now with this new investigation. I suppose that's all the more reason to get going on hiring someone new," Sam said.

"True." Jo seemed as enthused as Sam, and they both looked toward the corner where Tyler's old desk sat.

Sam's stomach growled. "I'm heading to Holy Spirits for a burger."

At the word burger, Lucy snapped her head up hopefully. Sam looked down and laughed. "Yes, I'll get you one too." Then he looked at Jo. "Do you want to join me?"

"Can't tonight," Jo said. "I promised Finn I'd go scout out new homes for him. But I gotta finish this paperwork first, so I'll stay and keep Lucy company for a while."

CHAPTER SEVENTEEN

Sam left Lucy at the police station in her big fluffy dog bed. Lucy looked disappointed that she couldn't go with him, but the promise of bringing back a burger seemed to mollify her, and she had Jo to keep her company at least for a little while.

Holy Spirits wasn't very crowded, and Sam took his usual seat at the bar. Billie slid a Mooseneck in front of him, and he put in his order for a plain burger for Lucy and an Old-Man-In-The-Mountain burger for himself. The burger, which consisted of bacon, caramelized onions, and some kind of secret sauce, had been named after the outcropping of rock in Franconia Notch that resembled a man's face. When Sam was a little kid, his parents had taken him countless times to marvel at the big rock that jutted out from the cliff and could be seen from the main road. It was a big tourist attraction until it crumbled and fell down in 2003. Now it was just a big rock.

"Hey, what's up?" Mick slapped him on the shoulder and slid into the seat beside him. Leaning his strong forearms on the bar, he waved two fingers at Billie. Billie must've seen him come in and was already pouring the Jack Daniel's into the small tumbler.

"Oh, you know, same old stuff. Murder, corruption, idle threats from Thorne." Sam swigged his beer and watched Mick's blue eyes widen.

"Idle threats?" Mick asked.

"I don't know if you heard, but Mike Donnelly was shot. I think it was set up to look like a suicide, but it wasn't. Margie says Thorne was after him for his land."

"Doesn't mean he killed him," Mick said as Billie slid the burger in front of Sam. "Though I wouldn't put it past him."

"Right. Well, thing is, I went and talked to him, and he made a weird threat. He alluded to knowing what happened twenty years ago." Sam took the bun off the burger and spread the sauce around just the way he liked it, making sure the brown strings of onion were spread out to cover the whole top of the burger. Then he put the bun back on and took a bite. It was juicy, savory, and tangy.

"You mean with Gracie?" Mick asked.

"Uh-huh. What else could it be? He specifically mentioned twenty years ago, and he mentioned it had something to do with Dupont." Sam took another bite and chewed while they both thought about it. "How could either one of them possibly know anything?"

Mick stared into his drink as he swirled it around, the ice cubes clinking against the side of the glass. "I don't know. Dupont went to Harvard. Two of the rapists were from Harvard. But we looked into that. He didn't know them."

"Not that we could find," Sam said. "Maybe we overlooked something. We were younger, less experienced, and emotional about defending Gracie."

Mick's face softened. "How is Gracie?"

Sam's heart twisted. His cousin Gracie had been a promising singer down in Boston twenty years ago when she'd been brutally raped by four college students. Even though two decades had gone by, the effects still showed. She was a hermit that barely left her house. Her music career had ended that night. The girl was afraid of her own shadow now, and Sam couldn't do anything to help her.

"I haven't seen her in a while." He made a mental

note to visit her the next day. Maybe Lucy would cheer her up. His cousin was skittish around people but hadn't lost her trust in animals.

Sam finished the rest of his burger in silence. What did Dupont know about what he and Mick had done to avenge Gracie? Gracie's memory about that day was fuzzy. She vaguely remembered what had happened to her when they'd found her unconscious next to the Charles River. She couldn't even name her assailants, only to tell them it was four boys and one had a crimson scarf.

They'd never uncovered any evidence that Dupont was even remotely involved. Could they have missed something?

"I don't know. Dupont is sleazy and all, but I don't think he's a rapist," Mick said as if reading Sam's mind.

"You never really know what people are capable of. Most of us are keeping secrets." Sam's thoughts turned to Tyler and the extra twenty grand in his bank account. "How are things going with Tyler's investigation?"

Mick shook his head. "I've been keeping an eye on the grandson while I've been doing other business. He's acting a little skittish and jiggy. I think something's about to break."

"We discovered that Tyler had twenty thousand deposited in his account two weeks before he died."

Mick's brows shot up. "Twenty thousand?"

Sam nodded.

"You think he was into something?"

"I've no idea. But it's looking more and more like his death wasn't just a coincidence. Someone had a specific reason for wanting Tyler dead."

CHAPTER EIGHTEEN

The next morning, Sam was up early. The hunting camp he'd inherited from his grandfather felt quiet and empty without his daughters. But they had their own lives down in Massachusetts, and he had to respect that. Since he had no intention of inviting anyone to live with him, he'd mostly gotten used to the emptiness, except for the few days after his daughters visited. Now that he had Lucy, he didn't need much else.

He fiddled around in the kitchen, feeding Lucy and sipping coffee while he stared at the taxidermy that hung on the log walls. The deer-head mount and colorful lake trout brought back childhood memories. They had all been caught by his grandfather, who had taught him to fish and hunt.

The camp had creeped his last wife out, but to Sam it felt comfortable and homey. He hadn't done much to it, and it was still decorated much the way it had been in his grandmother's time, though she'd died over a decade ago. She'd been an outdoorswoman herself and favored a more camp-like decor. There were precious few feminine touches except for her favorite china teacups, her old batter bowls, and her own grandmother's flow blue china.

Not too many women would want to live in a camp like this, at least not according to Sam's second wife, who had refused to move there when he'd inherited it upon his grandfather's death. She'd insisted they buy a big old Victorian closer to town. He'd gotten rid of that Victorian shortly after getting rid of the wife. He'd never wanted to live there anyway.

He loved the cabin because it was stuffed with memories of his parents and grandparents, but most of all he liked the seclusion. The property was situated on twenty acres and teeming with wildlife. Owls, woodpeckers, foxes, and even some bears whose claw marks could be seen at the stand of beech trees that sat a little further into the woods. His favorite, the deer, came to the edge of the pond across the street in the summer right at dusk.

The police radio he kept next to the birch-framed

picture of his daughters on the bookshelf that divided the kitchen from the rest of the cabin squawked. The White Rock police department was too small to man the police station twenty-four, seven. They switched off with the state police and county sheriff at night and kept in communication by police band radio.

This morning, the radio was announcing a dispute over on Mooseridge Road. Sam answered the call then rinsed his coffee cup in the sink, whistled for Lucy, and headed out in the Tahoe.

The dispute was between longtime residents Ives Collier and Peter Demming. Peter complained that one of Ives's milking cows had trampled his fence. It took Sam twenty minutes and a couple of Bavarian cream donuts to get the two to shake hands and come to a friendly agreement over the fence. Peter even got a gallon of fresh milk out of the deal.

On the way back to the station, Sam decided to detour and visit his cousin Gracie. His conversation with Mick the night before had been a guilty reminder that he hadn't seen her in a while.

Gracie lived in an old Colonial with her parents. The house dated to the 1870s and had a large barn that still smelled of horses. Gracie loved the barn. It was her escape. She sat in there and played music.

Even though she didn't have an audience anymore, she still loved playing.

Today, she wasn't playing music, though she was in the barn. She sat in an old chair in the corner, watching a small TV. Her face lit with a smile when she saw Sam, and for a moment he got a glimpse of the happy-go-lucky person she'd been before the attack.

Sam had the urge to hug her, but he knew Gracie couldn't stand to be touched anymore. Once, she'd been very affectionate, but the rapists had stolen that from her.

Her eyes fell on Lucy, and her smile widened. "I heard you got a K-9."

Lucy trotted over, and Gracie crouched down to pet her. She was cautious at first. Lucy leaned into her, nudging her gently, her tail swishing happily as if she sensed Gracie needed encouragement. Gracie hugged the dog, and Sam saw a look of joy on his cousin's face, something he'd rarely seen in the past twenty years.

"How's the police business?" Gracie stood, reached into the college-sized fridge, and pulled out a soda. She held it toward him. "Soda?"

"No, thanks." Sam preferred coffee. "Police business is the same as usual. Busy, though, since we're down one guy."

Gracie nodded and watched Lucy as she made her way around the perimeter of the barn, sniffing every nook and cranny. She must've been having a field day, because Sam himself could smell the sweet scent of hay and old leather even though horses hadn't been kept in the barn for a hundred years. But the floors were worn from years of housing horses, and he could still see the chew marks on the low stall doors. Gracie motioned him toward the gable end of the barn, where there was a big window that overlooked the field.

They sat in the chairs and chatted. Gracie's attention span was short, her eyes always on the move, nervously darting toward the door and the dog. Her eyes lit on the TV behind him and widened. Her body stiffened. Sam turned around. Dupont's commercial was playing on TV.

"Mayor Dupont." He turned back to Gracie. "Do you know him?"

Gracie shook her head, her eyes still glued to the TV. "He's a bad man."

"Did you know him when you were down in Boston? He went to Harvard," Sam said.

At the mention of Harvard, Gracie's eyes jerked toward Sam, and his heart pinched. Of course the name of the college that the rapists had gone to would stir bad memories in her. He felt like a jerk for mentioning it.

Her brows mashed together. "I don't know. It's all such a blur from back then. I mean, I know him from White Rock, but I get a funny feeling when I see him." Her eyes flicked from the television to Sam. "Someone like him shouldn't be mayor."

"I couldn't agree more."

Sam watched his cousin cautiously. He wanted to delve deeper, ask more about Dupont and if she remembered him being around the boys that raped her. But thinking about that time was still painful for her, and she still couldn't even remember if she'd known the boys. Her testimony at the time was that she'd only seen them vaguely in the bar.

As if sensing Gracie's agitation, Lucy trotted over and stuck her head under Gracie's hand. Patting the dog seemed to calm her. Sam didn't want to make her upset again.

Was it possible Dupont had somehow been involved back then? He hadn't been with the boys that had done that to Gracie--Sam was sure of it. But why would he keep taunting him about it, and why would he wait until now?

Dupont knew something, and judging by Gracie's reaction, Sam thought there might be more to his involvement. If anyone could find out, it was Mick, and Mick had a vested interest in discovering whatever Dupont had on Sam, because whatever he had on Sam was also going to be bad news for Mick.

Sam's phone pinged with a text, and he took it out of his pocket. It was Reese.

Come on back to the station. I have interesting news.

CHAPTER NINETEEN

Twenty minutes later, Sam and Lucy were standing in front of the receptionist desk in the foyer of the police station. Jo and Reese were behind the desk, looking down at Reese's computer.

"I did a little digging around, looking into the Donnellys' finances like Jo asked me," Reese said.

"Good thinking." Sam hadn't asked Jo to do that, but it was something that needed to be done.

"Well, you never know what you might find. It's standard procedure, right?" Jo asked.

"Did you get a subpoena already?" Sam asked. If she had, she must've done it before Sam had threatened Thorne. Because Sam was sure Thorne would've gone to Dupont, and Dupont would've used his connections with the judge to stop any subpoenas if he was involved.

Reese plastered an innocent look on her face. "Of course. Well, I mean, one is coming, so I just expedited things."

Sam frowned. Reese was a whiz with computers, and she'd made a lot of contacts at the police academy who had a variety of useful skills. Sometimes cutting corners was necessary to get the job done quicker, but sometimes it bit you in the ass later on. Apparently it was too late now--they'd already found something, and judging by the looks on their faces, Sam knew it was something good.

Reese pushed a white donut bag out of the way and swung the computer around to face Sam. There were two windows up on her screen. She stood up and leaned over, her dark hair falling in front of her face as she pointed at one of the windows. "This is Mike Donnelly's bank account. The one his wife knows about."

It looked like the online dashboard of a regular bank account, just like Sam's. There wasn't much money in it. There was a checking account and a savings account, but neither of them showed a large balance, and the checking account looked to have normal deposits and withdrawals.

His eyes drifted to the other window, where Reese was tapping a cherry-red-polished nail. "This is his other bank account. The one his family doesn't know about."

"What do you mean they don't know about it? How do you know that?"

"It was opened two months ago and only has cash deposits. And here is the documentation." Reese pulled up another window that showed the paperwork with only Mike's signature.

"Makes sense Mike would have to open it on his own. Margie was probably too sick to go down to the bank and open an account," Sam said.

"Sure. But why would Mike be opening one now? With his wife so sick, you'd think he'd have other concerns," Jo said. "And where is this cash coming from? With Margie's obvious bills, where would he be getting the extra money to deposit?"

Sam looked at the screen again. It wasn't a lot of money. A thousand here. Five hundred there. According to the list of transactions, he would make a few deposits then withdraw most of it. "What do you think he's doing with the withdrawals?"

Reese tapped on the first window again. "It doesn't appear in this bank account, so he's not depositing it."

"Which means he's not using it to pay any of the medical bills or household bills," Jo said.

"Well then, *what* is he doing with it?" Sam asked.

"That, I can't help you with," Reese said then looked out the door. "Oh, shoot."

The door opened, and a nervous-looking young man walked in.

"Can I help you?" Sam asked.

Reese had jumped up from her desk and grabbed a piece of paper from the printer. She shoved it into Sam's hand. It was a resume. "I forgot to tell you. This is Walker Johnson. His interview for the open position is scheduled right now."

CHAPTER TWENTY

Kevin had been out all day, taking one annoying call after another. First it was Mrs. Achison, who had a cat stuck in a tree. He was still picking splinters out of his palm from using her rickety old ladder that looked as if it dated to about 1910. The cat had been cute, though, a fluffy gray kitten with big round green eyes. And Mrs. Achison had been appreciative, but getting cats out of trees wasn't exactly the reason he'd gotten into police work.

He'd also sorted out a dispute involving Julian Martin, whose sheep had gotten loose and eaten Gloria Williams' daisies. They were prized daisies that she was cultivating for some sort of contest. He managed to smooth it over by getting Julian, a confirmed bachelor, to take Gloria, a widow, to dinner.

When he got back to the station, Sam was interviewing for Tyler's replacement. Kevin didn't know how he felt about that. He'd been offered the full-time job but had refused it, and now he was starting to wonder if he'd made the right decision.

As long as he was part time, he'd always be different from the others. But wasn't that good? If Sam and Jo were up to something shady, maybe he was better off to disassociate himself from their activities as much as he could.

"You save the cat?" Jo was tapping her pencil on her desk blotter, her feet up on the edge of the desk, leaning back, relaxed.

"Yep. Cute kitten." Kevin nodded toward Sam's office. "Another applicant?"

"Yep."

"What do you think?"

Jo shrugged. "Takes me a while to get warmed up to people."

That was no exaggeration. Kevin had been working with Jo for over a year now, and she was just barely starting to thaw out. He suspected she had some skeletons in her closet, but she wasn't the type to go blabbing about them. She was one of those people that kept things to themselves.

"Anything new on the Donnelly case?" Kevin asked. He'd already worked thirty hours this week and was feeling tired from it. He hoped that there was nothing new. He didn't want more work. But his contact had asked him to work closely with Sam and Jo so as to keep informed on this case.

"Seems the guy had a secret bank account," Jo said.

"Secret bank account? Why would someone have one of those?" Kevin asked.

"Apparently he's got a secret," Jo said. "Maybe a secret that got him killed."

"So what was he doing with the money?" Kevin asked.

"That's the thing. We don't know. We can see cash deposits, and then he makes withdrawals, but we don't know what he does with them. They don't go into his regular bank account."

Kevin frowned. One of the things his contact had asked him to do before was find out where Tyler was going after he made withdrawals. It had turned out Tyler was only going to the medical center, which ended up being something related to his sister's illness. But in order to find that out, Kevin had used a method suggested by his contact. Something that he'd seen on a television show, of all places.

"How does he withdraw the money from the bank?"

Jo frowned down at the paper on her desk. "Looks like he uses the ATM on the corner of Main and Berkeley."

"Hold on." Kevin sat at his computer and typed on the keyboard. Most ATM machines had a camera that took video of transactions. He pulled up the document he had stored that showed which ATMs in town had that capability. If he was lucky, the one on the corner of Main and Berkeley had one. He was lucky.

"Check this out." Kevin swiveled the screen toward Jo, and she got up from her desk and came over. "This shows the ATM machines with video capability. I don't know how often they record over the videos, and it only turns on to record the transaction and shuts off pretty quickly, but I was thinking if Mike had someone with him when he made these withdrawals, then it might be on video."

Jo leaned over to get a better look at the screen. "Can we get the video from that machine? Because if there was someone with Mike, that means they knew about this money, and *that* means that we need to talk to them."

SAM LEANED back in his chair as he smiled at the nervous applicant, Walker Johnson, sitting across from him. He went through the motions of the interview, asking where he had worked, what kind of work he liked to do best, what his biggest case was. But the whole time, Sam's mind was on his cousin Gracie's reaction to Dupont and the fact that Mike had a bank account with suspicious activity.

He wouldn't have been so suspicious of the bank account if it hadn't just been opened two months before. Lots of people had bank accounts separate from their spouse, but with Margie being so ill, it didn't sit right with Sam. Why open a bank account like that when she was going to be gone soon, anyway? The only reason he would be doing it now was he was doing something he didn't want Margie-- or his kids--to know about.

Was it possible he was taking money from Thorne somehow? But why? Maybe he had promised the land to Thorne but didn't want to actually go through with the deal until Margie was gone. It would make sense that he wouldn't want to upset her in her condition. And maybe someone was giving him money in advance to seal the deal and give Mike something to pay off those medical bills. But if that were the case, how come the money never made it into the account from which they paid those bills, and why were the amounts so small?

"And I'm a crackerjack at filing," the eager kid said, his Adam's apple bobbing up and down.

Sam's attention jerked back to the interview. "Have you ever been out in the field on a case?" Sam asked.

Walker twisted his hands nervously. "I pulled over a couple of speeders, and I helped settle a dispute down at the Piggly Wiggly."

"A dispute?"

"Yes, sir. It seemed Mrs. Winters walked out with a ham she didn't pay for. Mr. Peabody chased her right into the parking lot. But Mrs. Winters, well, she was getting on in years, and her memory wasn't so good. She thought she paid for it."

"I see. So you didn't have to draw your weapon?" Sam joked.

Walker scowled and looked at Sam. "Weapon? I wouldn't pull my weapon on Mrs. Winters."

Obviously, Walker was inexperienced and didn't have a sense of humor. Sam didn't see how the poor guy would fit in, but it was his second interviewee. How many would he have to go through before he would find one that was suitable? Maybe he should reconsider the first guy. He was better than this one.

Sam leaned back and steepled his fingers while Walker rambled on about his exploits at the Piggly Wiggly. Seemed they had a lot going on down in Lewis at that store. Sam's mind wandered to more interesting things like what everyone else was doing out in the squad room. Probably researching something much more interesting than what he was doing in here.

Finally, Walker stopped, and Sam leaned forward in his chair. "Well, I think that about does it."

Sam stood even though the kid had a confused look on his face.

"Don't you want to hear about my filing system? The chief in Lewis says it's one of the best. That place was a mess when I came, and I really revolutionized the files."

"Maybe on the next interview," Sam said. Walker's face turned hopeful at the prospect of a second interview, and a pang of guilt shot through Sam. There wasn't going to be any second interview. Sam put a guiding hand on Walker's shoulder and led him toward the door. "Thank you for your time. We'll be in touch."

"Thank *you*," Walker said enthusiastically then turned to Kevin, Jo, and Reese, who were hunched over Kevin's computer, gave them an awkward salute, and left. Lucy, who was lying in her comfortable dog bed in the corner of the room, barely raised an eyebrow.

"How did that go?" Jo looked up from the computer. "Are you bringing him back to have me talk to him?"

Her words sounded sincere, but the look on her face told Sam she didn't want to talk to the guy. He thought about toying with her but had mercy.

"Not unless you want to hear about how he almost arrested a forgetful senior citizen who walked out with a ham at the Piggly Wiggly," Sam said. "I don't think he's gonna be a good fit."

But they'd already turned back to the computer. Reese was seated at Kevin's desk, her fingertips clacking on the keys while Kevin and Jo stared over her shoulder.

"What are you guys doing?"

"Kevin had a great idea," Jo shot over her shoulder. At her compliment, Kevin's cheeks turned crimson. "I printed out the bank statements of Mike's secret bank account. He made his withdrawals from the ATM on the corner of Main and Berkeley Street. Always the same ATM."

"That's interesting," Sam had come over to stand next to them and was looking down at the computer, where he could see a video running with an odd fish-bowl-like view of the street. "Is that some kind of surveillance video?"

"Yep. It's from the ATM. Kevin thought of it. And Reese..." Jo's voice drifted off. "Well, let's just say she talked to one of her friends and was able to expedite getting the video."

Sam simply sighed. Normally, getting a video like that would take time, but they didn't have time, so he wasn't going to argue. "So what's on it?"

"Check it out. We got lucky. Usually, they record over the video in a loop, but Mike made a withdrawal the day he was killed, and they hadn't looped over it yet."

Sam bent down to look at the screen. In the distorted video, he could clearly see Mike collect his money and turn away then walk across the street. "That's Mike withdrawing the money?"

"Yeah." Kevin sighed and leaned back in his chair. "We were hoping that someone might be with him and it would give us a lead, but he came alone, so it was a waste of time."

Sam's eyes were still on the screen. Mike's car-- the brown Ford Taurus--sat on the side street north of the ATM, but Mike was heading in the other direction. "Wait a minute, maybe he didn't have anyone with him at the ATM, but..."

Sam watched as Mike crossed the street and

headed toward another car parked on the side street next to the bakery. For a second, he veered out of the line of vision of the ATM, but then he reappeared and got into the passenger seat of the car.

"We didn't watch it long enough," Reese said. "He was meeting someone, and they're in a white Jetta!"

The video flicked off, and then the next person was at the ATM. Reese rewound and stopped on the part where Mike got into the car.

Kevin crouched forward, squinting at the screen. "But we can't see who's driving."

Reese tried enlarging the screen, but it was no dice. They couldn't see inside, especially with the angle and the bad quality of the video.

"Maybe I can have one of the guys I know at school try to enhance this?" Reese said.

"I don't think that'll be necessary." Sam leaned over and fiddled with the arrows until the screen was focused on the front of the car.

"There's the plate number plain as day. Run that number, and we may be one step closer to the killer."

CHAPTER TWENTY-ONE

The car belonged to a Judy Kendler, who lived on Lower Quail Road just out of town. Too bad Judy died six months ago. Could whoever was using her car be involved with Thorne?

Sam and Jo drove out to the house as a thunderstorm came through. They could see the dark clouds rolling in as they drove up Wolf Hill, and the landscape dropped away to give them a view of the valley with the river below. The sound of thunder echoed across like a giant drumming on a kettledrum. Fat raindrops splatted onto the windshield.

Jo had put her sunglasses on the dashboard, and she held the yellow smiley mug in her lap. Her green eyes appeared luminous in the dark light of the storm. Sam could smell the ozone in the air. A bolt of lightning zigzagged to the ground in the distance, lighting up the sky for a split second. Then another crash of thunder echoed.

"I think we should leave Lucy in the car." Jo glanced back at the dog, who was crouched on the floor in front of the backseat. "I don't think she likes thunderstorms."

"Apparently not," Sam said. There hadn't been a thunderstorm since they'd adopted Lucy as part of the K-9 unit, but the dog looked completely terrified. "It might get dangerous in there anyway." Sam automatically glanced to make sure Jo had her gun belt. "I wouldn't want Lucy to get hurt."

Jo glanced toward their cargo container in back where they kept the police-issue bulletproof vests. "You think we should suit up?"

"No. Bulletproof vests might spook him. We can just go in and act friendly. I figure if it's one of Thorne's thugs, he'll run out the back doors as soon as he sees us. Usually they're not brave enough to be confrontational and prefer to run away," Sam said. Hopefully this one wouldn't be one of the few that preferred a fight.

Judy Kendler's house was a small 1960s ranch style with a porch running along the front that looked as if it had once been lovingly cared for but had recently fallen into neglect. The paint still looked fresh, and someone had made an attempt to mow the lawn, but the lines made by the mower were uneven. The flower beds had weeds sprouting up in between last year's mulch. The white Jetta was in the driveway.

Sam and Jo ran from the car to the porch. At least that provided some shelter from the rain, though they got soaked in the process. Sam knocked on the door. They heard a rustle inside, and he tensed, his hand hovering over his gun.

A young man of about seventeen answered the door. His eyes flicked from Sam to the police car and reflected fear masked by hostility. "Can I help you?"

"Is this the residence of Judy Kendler?" Sam asked.

The kid crossed his arms across his chest, his face hardening. "What of it?"

The kid was acting brave, but Sam sensed fear rippling underneath.

"Are you a relative?" Sam asked.

"I'm her son."

"What's your name?"

"Tommy. I haven't done anything wrong. The payment is in the mail. So I'm not sure why you're here."

He tried to shut the door, but Sam stuck his foot in it.

The boy scowled as he looked down.

Behind them, the rain pelted on the driveway. Hail had started and was pinging off the white Jetta.

"That's your mom's car, right?" Sam asked.

"Yeah."

"Who's been driving it?"

Tommy's eyes narrowed. "What business is it of yours? I have the right to drive it. Mom made up a will before she died."

Tommy's words had a hardness to them that didn't match the look in his eye. The kid wasn't as tough as he was putting out.

"Look, son, you can answer our questions here, or I can take you down to the police station. Which do you prefer?"

Tommy stepped back, and Sam and Jo went in. The inside matched the outside. The furniture was well kept but about a decade old. The living room had a bookcase on one wall, the shelves layered in dust. The television was on, and a puffy comforter lay on the couch. A box of cereal stood open on the coffee table. Next to it, a spoon sat in a bowl. The bowl had a shallow pool of milk on the bottom with some soggy cereal floating in it.

From what they'd found out back at the police station, Judy Kendler had been unmarried. Sam couldn't tell if Tommy was enjoying his new non-parental life, or if Judy had done everything for him and he was just now trying to figure out how to get along on his own.

Tommy didn't invite them in farther, so the three of them stood just inside the door. "What are your questions? I can live here. I have a job. I can pay the bills."

"Who has been driving the white Jetta?" Jo asked.

Tommy swiveled his head toward her. "No one but me. What's that got to do with anything?"

"You haven't loaned the car to anyone? A family member, maybe?" Sam asked.

"No." Now Tommy was starting to get that look on his face. That look that told Sam he was lying. The same look that told Sam to be cautious because from here on out anything could happen. He knew from many interrogations that once the suspect was caught lying, their anger could turn on a dime. He glanced over at Jo and knew she was thinking exactly the same thing.

"Then if you haven't loaned the car to anyone, maybe you'd like to explain why it was at Mike Donnelly's camp and why he was seen handing over money to you on Main Street."

Uncertainty flickered in Tommy's eyes. "What do you mean?"

Sam stepped a little closer, and Tommy backed up. Not so cocky now that Sam had discovered that he was at the Donnellys' camp. "So you were there? And he did meet you in town to give you money? Were you blackmailing him?"

The boy stepped back, holding his hands up. "No. I wasn't doing that."

Sam took another step toward him. "Or maybe you were selling him drugs for his wife's cancer? I hear pot can help with symptoms, and maybe you got your supply from Thorne and passed some along."

Tommy looked scared now. "What? I'm not a drug dealer!"

"But you do work for Thorne, right? That's why you were at Mike's camp?"

"What?" Was Tommy playing dumb? He looked genuinely confused.

"You need money." Sam gestured to the house. "Your mom left a bunch of bills. You need to pay the mortgage. The car loan."

Tommy nodded. "But I have two jobs. I can pay the bills. Plus, I have some money from..."

His voice drifted off. Sam moved in for the kill, stepping even closer so now he was in Tommy's face. Tommy had nowhere to go. The backs of his legs were already against the sofa.

"That's right. You have money from Thorne. You were desperate. With your mom gone and no money, you'd be out on the street. Thorne offered you money to do his dirty work. So you went to Mike Donnelly's camp and killed him."

Tommy collapsed back onto the sofa. His wide eyes darted from Sam to Jo. "Is that why you're here? You think I killed Mike Donnelly?"

"Exactly. He was seen getting into your car last week, and your car was at his camp the very night he died. If you confess now and tell us who was behind it, we'll go easy on you. Maybe you won't get the death penalty."

Tommy burst into tears, his hands covering his face. Sam had never seen a killer cry quite so emotionally before. He glanced at Jo, who had a funny look on her face. She gave a half shrug. Apparently, Tommy's behavior was a new one on her, too.

Sam looked down at him, his voice gentle now. "It's going to be okay. Just tell us what you know about why Thorne wanted you to kill Mike Donnelly."

Tommy shook his head violently. In between sobs, he blurted out, "I didn't kill him. Why would I? I loved him. Mike Donnelly was my father."

CHAPTER TWENTY-TWO

All the cockiness had gone out of Tommy, and now Sam thought he looked more like a lost little boy than a murder suspect. Jo had taken pity on him and sat him in the kitchen while she rummaged in the cabinet for tea.

Sam had never seen Jo do any mothering before. He'd always thought of her more as the type that liked to shoot first and be comforting later, but this nurturing role kind of suited her. Not for the first time he reflected on how different Jo was from any of his ex-wives. They'd been more... girly. Something Sam knew nothing about. Jo wasn't girly at all, yet she exuded an attractiveness that men seemed to like. Jo seemed to be oblivious to the fact that she turned men's heads. Maybe that was part of what made her so appealing.

Watching her, Sam felt a strange spark that he hadn't felt in a long time. A spark he didn't want to feel. Especially not about Jo. Sam and Jo's relationship wasn't along those lines, and he wanted to keep it that way. They were friends and worked together. They trusted each other. In fact, he trusted her almost as much as he trusted Mick. But that was as far as it went. Sam didn't have room in his life for a serious relationship, and he liked Jo too much to take it any further when he knew it wasn't anything that would last.

Tommy stopped crying, and they sat around the small kitchen table while he wrapped his hands around the comforting mug of tea. Outside, the rain tapped a steady rhythm on the windows as Tommy sniffled into a tissue.

"Mom always said my father took off. I never knew until she died. She got cancer. Went quick." More sniffles. "She left me a note telling me that Mr. Donnelly was my father and I should contact him. She didn't leave any money, and she was worried about me. Maybe she thought Mr. Donnelly would support me. I don't know."

"And what happened when you contacted him?" Jo asked.

"At first he didn't believe me. But he'd had an

affair with my mom, I guess, and he did the math. My mom moved away when she first got pregnant with me and didn't come back for five years. Apparently, he never guessed he was my father. She never told him because he was married at the time."

"So you kind of had a secret relationship with him?" Sam asked.

Tommy shrugged. "We got a DNA test to prove it. He was a nice guy. He wanted to tell his family, but his wife was so sick, he didn't think it was the right time. He was waiting for her to go, and then he would tell the other kids gently. My half brother and sister, I guess." Fresh tears formed in his eyes as he looked around the house. "I was looking forward to that because I don't have anyone else. It was just me and Mom. So, you see, I wouldn't have killed my dad because now I have no one."

Sam wondered about that. He did seem sincere, but Tommy could always try to connect with his half brother and sister. If he did have a DNA test, he could prove they were related. But something gnawed at him. Obviously, Tommy needed money. Sam wondered if Tommy would benefit financially from Mike's death. "When we first came, you thought we were here to repossess the house or the car, didn't you?"

Tommy nodded. "My mom didn't have any life insurance, and there were a lot of bills left over to pay. What little she had only covered that. I have a little, but she couldn't work that last month. She was behind on the mortgage. I have a job at Charlie's Restaurant and a second job at the hardware store, and I'm working to pay off what we owe. But I was afraid I would get it all taken away. And the money from Mike was helping."

Sam had seen the withdrawals from Mike's account, and they didn't add up to a lot. If Tommy's mom was behind and there had been medical bills, that wouldn't be nearly enough. "Where did he get this money?"

"I don't know. He said something about selling things off. I didn't want to take the money, but when he saw my bills piling up, he wanted to help. He couldn't let his family know, so sometimes we would meet at his cabin. He gave me a key for the gate in the road. And sometimes he would meet me at the ATM."

"How long had this been going on?"

Tommy shrugged. "About three months. I went to him a month or so after my mom died, but at first he didn't believe me. I wasn't gonna keep bugging him if he didn't want me. But then I guess he thought about it, did the math, and came to me."

"So you *were* there the day he died?" Jo asked. "Witnesses saw a white Jetta."

Tommy sucked in a stuttered breath. "I was there. I just wish I'd stayed longer. Then I might've been able to stop someone from killing him."

"So you're saying he was alive when you left?" Sam asked. "And what time was that?"

"Just after supper. Mike got me a ham salad sandwich from the deli. It's my favorite. Mom used to make a really good ham salad." Tommy's voice cracked, and he paused for a second then continued. "But I had to get to my second job at the hardware store and be there by six p.m."

That would be easy enough to check. "Was anyone else there at the cabin? Did you see anyone when you were leaving?"

Tommy shook his head. "I wish I had. Then I could help find my dad's killer. But when I left, he was there all alone."

"Was he upset or depressed?" Jo asked.

"No way. He was sad about his wife but had come to accept that. If you're asking about him killing himself like they said in the papers, I didn't see any sign of it."

"Did he ever talk to you about his will or anything?" Sam asked. If Tommy's alibi checked out, then he could rule him out as the killer, but if it didn't, money was a big motivator, and since Mike had known about Tommy for several months, he might have put something in his will already.

Tommy's eyes narrowed. "Oh yeah, I know all about wills now since Mom died. He did talk about it, and if you're thinking that he might've changed it so that I inherited something, he didn't. He knew his wife was dying, and he didn't want his kids somehow finding out that he changed the will until we had a chance to tell them about me. So, you see, I would've had no financial motive to kill him, either." Tommy turned pleading eyes on Sam. "Please promise me you won't tell his family about me. He didn't want them to worry, not right now. I know how it is when someone is sick because of my mom, and they don't need any added problems. I'd like to honor my dad's wishes on that. Besides, now that he's gone, I doubt his kids would want to have anything to do with me. Maybe it's for the best if they don't know at all."

Sam left it at that. It would be easy enough to check Tommy's alibi and to check the will. But if Tommy was telling the truth, that opened up another pool of suspects, especially if Mike wasn't the only one that knew about Tommy. Sam had to wonder if it was possible one of Mike's kids already knew they had a half brother. That would give him a new motive to explore in Mike's death. Because both Melody and Brian Donnelly would lose out if part of their inheritance went to Tommy.

CHAPTER TWENTY-THREE

The thunderstorm had passed by the time they were done talking to Tommy, and Lucy was sitting on the front seat, staring out the window at the door, waiting for them. She stood and wagged her tail happily as she watched them walk back to the car. Sam had cracked the window for Lucy--too bad he'd cracked the window on the passenger side, and Jo's seat was now soaking wet.

"You could've cracked one of the back windows." She opened the door and leaned in, taking some napkins out of the console and using them to sop up the seat. Good thing the Tahoe had leather seats-- cloth seats would've been a mess.

"Do you think Tommy was telling the truth?" Jo asked after they were on the road again.

"Easy enough to check out. If he was at the hardware store working that night, then we'll know he couldn't have killed Mike," Sam said. "But I believe him, don't you?"

"Yeah. I could tell at first he was nervous about something, but then once the truth came out, his whole demeanor changed. He was telling the truth." Jo pointed at the giant coffee cup sign for Brewed Awakening. "Can we stop for coffee?"

Sam had already put his blinker on. Jo got a bag of jelly donuts, and they both got coffees. At the drive-through, the girl gave them a treat for Lucy. Jo tossed into the backseat, and Lucy caught it and swallowed it whole.

"That's for being a good girl and staying in the truck." Jo settled into her seat and flipped the plastic lid on the Styrofoam cup. "Reese already requested a copy of Mike's will the other day. Hopefully, it's been faxed over. We'll see if he changed it. If not, then Tommy had no financial motive."

"But Melody or Brian might have," Sam said.

"Right. I thought of that too. But that means one of them must have known about Tommy. Do you really think they would be so cold blooded as to kill their father over that?"

Sam's gut tightened. "I hate to think it, but maybe it was more than just money. If one of them found out their dad had cheated all those years ago, the death might have had more to do with anger. And Brian did act a little off, don't you think?"

"Yep... But to kill his own father? Seems like it would make more sense that he would kill Tommy."

"You got a point there. Maybe he didn't intend on killing anyone. Maybe he confronted Mike with the fact that he found out he had a half brother and things escalated out of control," Sam said.

"Maybe. But how can we find out if Brian or Melody knew about Tommy? Tommy asked us to keep it a secret, and I feel like it's not up to us to let the cat out of the bag if they really didn't know," Jo said.

Sam pulled into the parking spot in front of the police station. "Maybe we won't have to let the cat out of the bag. Maybe there's another way for us to figure out if Mike's kids were involved. But first let's at least get a look at his will. If he did already change it, then that rules out the motive of these kids killing him for money."

"But not for passion." Jo hopped out of the truck then opened the side door to let Lucy out. "And if he did change it, then killing him might get Tommy a lot more money than those withdrawals Mike was making from that secret account."

"LEARN ANYTHING NEW?" Reese looked up from her computer, her fingers still typing on the keyboard as she looked up at Sam and Jo.

"We learned that Lucy is afraid of thunderstorms," Sam said.

Reese bent down and opened her arms, and the dog rushed over to her. "Oh, you poor thing." She rubbed Lucy's neck and then looked up at Sam. "Did the mean chief of police make you go outside in a thunderstorm?"

Lucy's tail swished back and forth as she settled into Reese's embrace, looking back at Sam and Jo reproachfully.

"At least we didn't make her go outside and get wet," Jo said, glancing at the back of her jeans, which were still wet from the seat.

"That nice man that sent you the postcard stopped by," Reese said.

Sam rolled his eyes. There was only one man she could be referring to. "Harry Woolston? He's no nice man. Don't hang around with him, and don't encourage him to come here."

Harry had been the chief of police in White Rock when Sam was a kid. He was retired now. Problem was, Harry got bored easily. If Reese encouraged him to drop by the station, the next thing they knew, he'd be insinuating himself into all of their cases and giving unwanted advice.

Reese frowned. "Well, he seemed nice."

"Oh yeah, he seems that way. Don't let that old guy fool you," Sam said. "Anyway, we were wondering if Mike's will came in. It turns out there's an interesting turn in the case."

Reese raised a brow. "The will did come in." She spun around and plucked something off the printer. "Here it is. Wife's will is there, too. What's the turn?"

No one else was in the station to overhear, so Sam told her. "Turns out Mike had an illegitimate son."

"Get out." Reese's eyes widened. "This is like a soap opera."

"Yeah, except it's real life. So don't let it get out. We don't want the family to get hurt. But the new revelation certainly adds a twist into our suspect list."

"You don't think this illegitimate son killed him, do you?" Reese asked.

"I'm not sure. He wouldn't benefit unless he's in the will, but it might've been the motivation for the kids. With Margie about to die and Thorne offering a lot of money for the land, it's starting to sound a little sticky. I'm not sure where to look." Sam held the papers up as he slipped around the post office box divider into the squad room. "Maybe there's something in here that will point us in the right direction."

CHAPTER TWENTY-FOUR

K evin pulled his Isuzu into a parking spot just a few down from the police station. Sam's Tahoe was back, so Sam and Jo must have already interviewed the suspect. Interviewing the suspect sounded a lot more interesting than the call Kevin had been on. Settling these minor disputes with the townies got old after a while.

He reached into his pocket, his fingers brushing against the plastic thumb drive. The drive had been empty according to his computer, but Reese had contacts, people with skills who might be able to find something hidden, and Kevin had a sneaking suspicion that something important might be hidden on there.

He knew he should hand it over to his contact. It had been found in Tyler's things, and they'd specifically said they were looking for data. But if Sam and Jo were on his side, shouldn't he hand it over to them? It might have to do with police work.

Never mind that they didn't have any unsolved cases or any information that was missing. Never mind that he didn't get to go and interrogate the suspect. He understood why Sam brought Jo. She was a sergeant. Kevin was just an officer. If anyone would do the detective work, it would be the highest-ranking officers, and it was Kevin's own fault that he hadn't gone up in rank because he'd chosen to work part time.

The money from his contact gave him enough that he didn't have to work full time, but Kevin was discovering it wasn't that satisfying to just take that money. He was starting to feel dirty. At first, they convinced him he would be helping to keep the police department free of corruption. Now, he wasn't so sure.

And today, he'd received a new note from his contact wanting more information. Kevin wasn't sure he wanted to give it.

Sam and Jo had started to include him, and it felt good. Sam had even said he'd done a good job.

But still Kevin suspected there might be some things Sam and Jo were doing that weren't exactly according to police procedure. Like, for example, the offhand remark he'd gotten when he went to his safety deposit box at his bank out in Colebrook earlier that morning. Maybe he was just being paranoid. The only way to find out was to ask Sam and Jo, and maybe he could use the thumb drive as sort of a way to prove to them that he was on their side, to become part of their inner circle.

Lucy trotted over to greet him as he opened the door, and his heart expanded. He had to admit he'd been wary of the large German shepherd mix at first, but he'd soon learned Lucy was a gentle creature, and since he connected better with animals than people, seeing Lucy was something he now looked forward to every day.

He pulled the thumb drive out of his pocket. It was the right thing to do to give it to Sam and Jo. He placed it on top of the folder he was carrying with the paperwork he had from the calls he'd been out on.

Jo and Sam were back in the squad room, looking at a piece of paper with Reese.

Sam looked up as he entered. "Hey, Kevin, did everything go okay?"

"Yeah, how about you? Did you get a confession?"

Sam laughed. "No such luck. Turns out it's even more complicated than we thought."

The phone rang, and Reese went back to her desk

in the reception area while Jo and Sam filled Kevin in on what had happened earlier.

They were talking to him just as they used to talk to Tyler. As if he was one of the gang. It made him feel confident, so he decided to ask them outright about the safety deposit box. "I was at the bank over in Colebrook this morning. I have an account there, and they told me to tell you that there was no safety deposit box? Is that something to do with this case? Did Mike have a safety deposit box you guys were looking into?"

Sam and Jo exchanged a sharp look that put Kevin's nerves on edge.

"No," Sam said. "Oh yeah. That's right." He looked at Jo. "Remember?"

"Right, we thought Mike might have a safety deposit box because he took that money out of the ATM and we didn't know what he did with all of it."

Kevin frowned. That couldn't be true. He'd been here the whole time when they'd looked at the ATM tape, and it was clear Mike had gotten into the white Jetta right afterward. Sam and Jo had interviewed Tommy right away, so they knew where the money was going. And even if they suspected Mike hadn't given it all to Tommy, Kevin doubted they would have had time to make their way to the bank in Colebrook, because they would have started looking at banks closer to home first. And, even if Mike *had* stashed more money, why would they care where it was after learning about Tommy?

But why would Sam and Jo lie about that? A chill came over him. His contact had been right--Sam and Jo were up to something, and it wasn't exactly legal.

He inconspicuously shoved the thumb drive into the pocket in the front of the folder.

"Was that something for me?" Sam nodded at the folder.

"Oh, this? No. Just the routine case stuff. I'm gonna go put it all into the computer now."

Kevin sat at his desk, glad that he hadn't told his contact he was done with spying. What had he been thinking, anyway? Of course Sam and Jo were including him in everything--they wanted to keep him from being suspicious. Because they were up to something shady on the side, just as Tyler had been.

Now he was glad he hadn't confided in them. He would've forfeited all that money and probably been taken down along with them in the process.

SAM WATCHED Kevin walk back to his desk. He could've sworn the officer was about to hand him something that was in his folder. Sam couldn't see much else but paperwork. Maybe it was his imagination, but Kevin's demeanor seemed to have changed while they were talking.

He glanced at Jo, and she was frowning at Kevin. It had been a big slipup that the person at the Colebrook bank had mentioned the safety deposit box to Kevin. Sam hadn't even thought about that when he and Jo had gone around pretending they were on police business while trying to find the box that fit Tyler's key. They'd have to be more discreet in the future. Even though Sam thought they might be able to trust Kevin, the fewer people that knew a lot about what they were doing, the better, especially in light of Tyler's big bank deposit. They might be into something that could get dicey.

"Hey, Sam, almost forgot you got an interview in fifteen," Reese yelled across the partition. Sam grimaced. He wished the whole interviewing process were over. He looked at Jo. "Maybe you could take this one?"

Jo made a face. "Maybe. Let's figure out this will thing first."

"Well, unfortunately, it could go either way. Here's how it's worded. He bequeaths all his stuff to Margie. If Margie predeceases him, the estate is to be split equally among his issue. It doesn't specifically name anyone, and with the DNA test, Tommy would clearly have an argument that he was Mike's issue. If Mike died after Margie, Tommy would have claim to one-third of his estate," Sam said.

"Then Tommy was right. He wouldn't have a reason to kill Mike. Quite the opposite, because Mike was already giving him money, but now that Mike is dead, that money will dry up. I assume Margie's will leaves everything to Mike, right?"

"Right. Which means Mike's kids could have a motive to make sure that Mike died before Margie did."

"*If* they knew about Tommy," Jo said.

"Good point. How would one of them find out?" Sam asked. "Melody was taking care of the mail. What if the bill for the DNA test came to the house and she found it?"

"We need to double check where Melody was that night. And Brian too. There was something funny going on with their alibis. Brian said he lives at those apartments across from the pharmacy--the Bluebell Arms--and he was home alone. Melody said she saw him, but I'm not sure I trust her. How can we verify Brian was at home in the Bluebell Arms apartments?" Jo asked.

A voice rang out from near the post office box partition. "That's easy. My friend Charlie Hobbs manages the place, and he knows everything that goes on there day and night. Nothing that happens escapes him. If your man was home, he'll know."

The voice belonged to Harry Woolston. He was tall and wiry, with a head full of thick white hair. He stood beside the partition, his keen blue eyes taking in every detail of the room.

Harry was pushing eighty but had a brain as sharp as a teenager's. Unfortunately, that meant that retirement didn't suit him. Harry got bored sitting around playing golf and bridge, and now that he was home for the summer, he wanted to insinuate himself into Sam's investigations.

Then again, in this case, it might not be such a bad idea. Sam knew how the good-old-boy network worked, and he knew that most folks didn't want to get involved and tended to be closemouthed with the cops. If Sam talked to the apartment building owner himself, he might not get any information, but with Harry along, he'd get the truth.

"Okay, Harry. We'll let you come with us to talk to this Charlie Hobbs, but that's it. You're not getting in on the case," Sam said.

"We'll see." Harry smiled, took his phone out of his pocket, held it at arm's length, and squinted. "Now let me remember how to work this thing."

The front door opened, and a young man of medium build walked into the lobby. He stopped at

Reese's desk. "I'm here for the interview. Wyatt Davis."

Harry's attention wavered from the phone, and he stepped to the side so he could look into the lobby. He glanced from Sam to Wyatt. "Well, you don't say. Come right in. We've been waiting to talk to you."

CHAPTER TWENTY-FIVE

It turned out that Harry was pretty good at interviewing. He asked all kinds of questions that Sam wouldn't have thought of. Questions that went beyond general police procedure and into the psyche of the applicant. Sam felt like taking notes so he could ask the same kinds of questions on future interviews.

When they were done and Wyatt had left, Sam turned to Harry. "So what do you think?"

"All you young people depend too much on computers and technology. I think you need to get someone in here who knows how to figure out who the killer is with his mind." Harry tapped the side of his head and leaned back in his chair. "But I suppose this one seemed okay. He wasn't too green around the gills, but he wasn't the gung-ho type that'll drive you crazy, either. I haven't talked to the other applicants, though, so I can't measure him against them. You want me to talk to them?"

Sam got up from his chair. He didn't want Harry to get too comfortable hanging around at the police station. He did agree with Harry that Wyatt seemed like the most likely candidate, but he'd have Jo talk to him and maybe bring some of the others in again just to be sure.

Lucy barked out in the squad room, and Sam opened the door to see Dupont standing there with a dog treat in his hand and Lucy raising her paw up in the air on his command. Lucy was becoming more trustful of Dupont--either that, or she was willing to overlook his personality flaws to get the treats.

Dupont straightened his blue Armani suit when he saw Sam, and his eyes drifted over to Harry behind him. "What brings you here? Are you in some kind of trouble?" Dupont asked.

Harry laughed. "Don't you start on me, Harley Dupont. I wouldn't be casting any stones if I were you."

Dupont's beady eyes got even beadier. "You're no longer the chief here, Woolston. You do realize that, I hope."

"Oh, I know you're the big fancy mayor and everything." Harry's criticism of Dupont ratcheted up

Sam's opinion of him. "But I gotta tell you there's a lot of us in town that don't like the way things are going here."

"What do you mean?" Dupont asked. "My popularity rating is higher than ever. People are seeing my commercials all over the county." He bent down to pet Lucy. "And with the addition of Lucy to the police force, the townspeople like me now more than ever."

"*Some* of the townspeople." Harry stepped closer to Dupont. "But there's some of us that see what you're doing. Some of us have noticed you're giving a little bit of extra favoritism to Thorne and his destructive building plans."

Dupont scowled. "I am not. I'm looking out for the economy of this town. Building restaurants and hotels brings in jobs."

"And it kills off wildlife and ruins the pristine landscape," Harry said.

"Some things must be sacrificed in the name of progress." Dupont turned to Sam. "Speaking of which, is there any progress on Mike Donnelly's case? I hope you aren't still going around harassing innocent citizens. Word is out that you are continuing to investigate, and people are getting nervous there is a murderer in our midst. Why aren't you ruling it a simple suicide?"

"We've got some things we need to look into before we can do that. The vultures did a job on the body, and we couldn't prove conclusively that Mike shot himself. We have to do our due diligence by law. Wouldn't want the taxpayers to think we did a shoddy job of investigating. So if you'll let us get back to it..." Sam's voice drifted off.

Dupont thought for a moment. It took a while for things to sink in with him. "Fine, I'll leave you to it. I just came to make sure that Lucy was being cared for properly by you people and that you weren't wasting taxpayer money on some kind of vendetta."

"You're one to talk about wasting taxpayer money." Harry stepped closer to Dupont. "Us senior citizens are watching you. We don't like the way all these new buildings are going up, and rumor has it Marnie Wilson is going to run against you, so you better watch it. She's got the senior vote, and up here, that counts for a lot. Us seniors don't want the woods all chopped up and newfangled hotels going up. We don't want anyone who is in bed with someone like Thorne running our town."

"I'm not in bed with anyone." Dupont became defensive. "I'm only looking out for the good of the town." And with that, he turned on his heel and left.

Harry smirked and turned to Sam. "I love getting his dander up. He was a jerk as a young man, and I see it hasn't changed much." Harry pulled out his phone and squinted at it again. "Now let me see if I can find Charlie's number. It's suppertime now, but I can see if I can get us an invite over to that apartment building so we can check out those alibis first thing tomorrow."

CHAPTER TWENTY-SIX

Harry's phone pinged immediately after he hung up with Charlie Hobbs, causing him to shuffle and juggle the phone comically until he finally got it answered. It was his wife, Mabel, who demanded he come home. Harry left them with the threat that he'd be back the next morning. Jo guessed even an important ex-chief of police had to answer to someone.

Kevin had already left, and Reese was packing up her desk. "Do you need me to stay and watch Lucy if you're going out for something to eat?" Jo asked.

"I'm heading straight home, so I'll take her," Sam said.

Reese hovered in the opening beside the post office boxes. "Do you need me to do anything else?"

"No, take off," Sam said.

Reese left, and now that they were alone in the station, Sam turned to Jo. "I know we've been busy with this investigation, but I was wondering if you found out any more about that deposit and Tyler's bank account."

"Nothing. The deposit was cash, so it's not traceable," Jo said.

"Kinda like how Mike had cash deposits," Sam said.

"Yeah, but I don't think the two are related." Jo tapped the end of her pencil against her lip. "He didn't withdraw it, so we can't look at an ATM video. Maybe we could get the bank surveillance tapes, but I'm not sure what we'd learn from that."

Sam sighed. "That would take a court order. We don't want anyone to know we're investigating."

"Speaking of which, we need to be a little bit more careful."

"Right. We don't want another slipup like we had with Kevin finding out we were at his bank. It's a catch twenty-two. If we don't pull our badges, no one will give us the information, and if we don't get the information, we may never find the box that the key unlocks."

They both glanced toward Sam's office, where the key sat inside his drawer.

"What if someone else knows about the key?" Jo

said. "Maybe someone else is looking for that key. Might be smart to hide it somewhere."

"Right. Now that we know about the cash deposit, we know he was up to something bigger than we thought before. In my drawer, though, I figure it's hidden in plain sight with all the other keys."

Jo glanced at the empty desk sitting in the corner. Tyler's desk. She thought Tyler had been like her and Sam. That he'd do anything for justice. But, as she'd discovered early on in her life, you never really knew what secrets someone else was keeping. "You're probably right."

"In the meantime, I have Mick trying to see if he can figure out what was going on with Tyler," Sam said.

"If anyone can figure it out, it'll be Mick," Jo said. "How is the interviewing going?"

Sam made a face. "Honestly, I don't really feel great about any of them. We worked so well together with Tyler, it's hard to think about anyone filling his shoes." Sam shrugged, glancing at the desk. "But now with what we're finding out, maybe we don't want someone to exactly *fill* them."

"What do you think about Kevin? He's been stepping it up lately, but then he acted kind of weird when he found out about that safety deposit box. I don't know if he would get on board with what we're doing. Should we let him in?" Jo asked.

Sam thought about that for a minute and then shook his head. "I don't know. I thought we could trust Tyler. I mean, we worked so closely with him, and look what we are finding out now. I don't get that same trust vibe from Kevin."

Jo nodded slowly. She felt the same way but didn't know if it was just her suspicious nature. "Best to keep things between ourselves for now and to apply more caution."

"Smart thinking."

Jo stood and started to gather her things. "I'm on call until eight o'clock tonight, so I'm gonna grab something from the diner and head home. You gonna be okay?"

"Yep. I'm heading home with Lucy. Gotta rest up. I'm sure Harry will be here first thing tomorrow morning." Sam rolled his eyes.

Jo laughed. "Awww. Let the guy have his fun. Soon enough, he'll be back in Florida and out of your hair."

"Sure. For now, I guess he does have his uses. He can get Charlie to talk to us and tell us the truth a lot better than we could on our own." Sam snapped his fingers, and Lucy trotted over to his side. "All right, I'm heading out. I'll have the CB band on in case something bad goes down. Remember I got your back."

Jo's heart warmed. Even though she and Sam were just friends, there was no one else she would trust more to have her back. It meant even more to her now in light of what they were discovering about Tyler.

"Thanks." Their eyes locked for a second, and something passed between them. Something she didn't understand. A deeper meaning to their friendship. Jo tore her eyes away. She was closer to Sam than she'd been to anyone in her adult life, but she couldn't handle their friendship being anything more than what it was now.

She grabbed her stuff and headed for the door.

SAM WAS on his second beer when the knock came on the screen door. Mick didn't bother waiting for an answer. He breezed in and helped himself to a beer from the fridge, just as he did every time he came to visit.

"Seems empty without the girls here." Mick echoed Sam's thoughts. Mick was somewhat of a surrogate uncle to Sam's daughters. Sometimes Sam wondered which one of them the girls liked better.

Of course, Mick had gotten to do all the fun parts without having to discipline them.

Mick squatted down to pat Lucy. "At least you got Lucy. You ever think about upgrading to something less hairy with two legs?"

"Only for a night or two. I'm not into long-term relationships anymore. What about you?"

Mick looked at him and winked and smiled the charming Mick Gervasi smile that had attracted all the girls during their younger years. Near as Sam could tell, it still worked, but Mick was a bit more selective now.

"Anyway, I assume you didn't come here just to talk about women," Sam said as Mick paced around the small cabin, looking at the pictures of Sam's family. Several generations were represented on the walls and in silver and birch-edged frames around the cabin. Mick paused in front of one that showed a fishing trip to Canada, just over the border. One of the many fishing trips Sam's dad and grandfather had taken him and Mick on when they were little boys. "How are your folks?"

Sam's folks were alive and doing well in Florida. They preferred the warmer climate to New England. Though sometimes they came back to visit in August--anything else was too cold for them. "Doing good. Dad's taking up golf. Mom's taking up painting."

"Sounds like my folks. You think we'll ever end up like that?" Mick sat down at the table and flicked the metal top from his beer so it spun like a coin on its side.

Sam made a face. "Nope."

Mick leaned back casually, but his face was serious. "I've been digging into that twenty grand. I don't know what Tyler was onto. My only lead is still the grandson of the woman whose car was stolen. I know he's got something to do with this."

Sam nodded. He felt the same. "It's just too much of a coincidence."

"But I can't get a handle on it. One thing is weird, though--he seems to be acting a little itchy, and from what I hear on the street, one of his friends has been missing for a while."

Sam's brow quirked up. "A while?"

Mick shrugged. "Honestly, I'm not making much headway on that." He reached into his back pocket and took out a piece of paper that had been folded a few times. He spread it flat on the table. It was a photocopy of an old newspaper picture. The debate team from Harvard. Mick tapped on one of the faces.

"Recognize this guy?"

"Dupont."

"And look who's here in this corner of the picture."

Sam's chest tightened. "Brendan Wright."

"Yep. Turns out Brendan and Dupont were on the debate team together back in college. None of the other guys involved in what happened to Gracie were on it. But this shows that Brendan knew Dupont, and even if it was just casually, I don't think it's any coincidence that Thorne is now putting the screws to you about what happened."

"No such thing as coincidences." Sam's mouth tightened into a grim line. "Do you think he told Dupont something about what happened that night? The night we went down to persuade Todd to tell the truth? Why would he?"

"It's gotta be something like that. You know Dupont--he's always trying to get something that he can use to his advantage later on. He knew we were poking around in Gracie's case--maybe he had something on Brendan or promised him something for information."

Sam leaned back in his chair. "That *is* how he operates. Maybe he pulled some strings on their jail sentence. He was connected even back then."

"Right. But why would he wait twenty years to bring it up?" Mick asked.

"Maybe he was waiting for the right time. The

whole time, he knew I was studying criminology. He knew I wanted to be chief of police here, and you know that even back then he was angling for a high political position either here in town or in the state Senate. I have been leaning on him about Thorne, so maybe he feels like now is the time to try to shut me up."

"He might look stupid, but he's pretty smart when it comes to saving his own skin," Mick said.

"Yeah, that's true, but it's a far cry from knowing something about someone and having evidence on someone. I doubt he'd have any actual evidence on us," Sam said.

Mick didn't look so convinced. "You know what they say--evidence can easily be fabricated. Maybe looking into this whole business with Tyler isn't such a smart idea. If Tyler was into something illegal and you get in the middle of it, it could implicate you somehow. If it has something to do with Dupont and Thorne, they could twist around anything you are doing to make it look like *you* are the one that is guilty. And with the way Dupont's acting, if I were you, I'd make sure I keep my nose clean from here on out."

CHAPTER TWENTY-SEVEN

Harry appeared at the police station the next morning with coffee and donuts for everyone. Reese gave Sam a look over Harry's shoulder as if to say, "See, he _is_ a good guy." Sam just shook his head. Reese had a lot to learn.

Sam and Jo grabbed a coffee and hopped into the Tahoe with Harry and Lucy in back. Jo scarfed a jelly donut on the way, dropping a red blob on her shirt.

Charlie Hobbs was almost the exact opposite of Harry Woolston. Where Harry was tall and thin and gangly, Charlie was short and fat. The two men greeted each other with a slap on the back.

"I see the new police still need help from us old-timers, eh?" Charlie smiled at Harry and side-eyed Sam as if he wasn't sure he could trust him. "You won't find much better than Harry when it comes to investigating."

Sam played along. "You don't say."

"I don't know how we ever solved any cases without him," Jo said dryly as she dabbed at the blob of jelly that now stained her light-blue button-down shirt. The dabbing only smeared it and made the stain bigger.

Lucy wagged her tail, sidling up against Harry. She'd taken a liking to him as they'd driven over together in the backseat of the Tahoe. Jo suspected Harry had been feeding her something from his pocket.

Charlie looked at Lucy. "I hope you're not going to do any of that search-and-seizure type stuff. I know those dogs can smell drugs. But I assure you there's none of that going on in my building."

They glanced at the building. It was a two-story brick construction that had six apartments in it. It was on one of the busier streets that housed mostly commercial businesses and old Victorians converted into apartment buildings and sat across from a big pharmacy.

Jo figured if Brian was living there, he probably didn't have very much money. For a guy in his thirties, she thought he would've been doing better.

She'd gotten the impression when they were at the Donnellys' house that he was hiding something. Maybe he'd just been embarrassed about his circumstances.

Whatever the case, Brian clearly needed money. His mother wouldn't be around for very long, but Mike had been in pretty good shape. Would Brian kill him so he could inherit his share of the estate? Thorne had mentioned one of the kids was champing at the bit to sell the farm. Had Brian been negotiating with Thorne on the side? And if so, maybe Mike's death had nothing at all to do with Tommy.

"So what do you need to know, Harry?" Charlie asked.

Harry looked at Sam.

Sam said, "We have a question about Brian Donnelly. We heard he lives here."

Charlie nodded and pointed to a window on the second floor. "Yep, right in Apartment 2b. I hope he's not in any trouble. He's a quiet lad."

"Don't know yet. We're trying to find out if he was here on Monday night, say around seven p.m.," Sam said. "Would you happen to know?"

"Of course I would," Charlie said. "I make it my business to know the comings and goings in my building. I run a clean shop here, and I need to keep tabs on things so they don't get out of hand. You know how young people are. They need constant supervision."

Harry nodded solemnly.

Charlie screwed up his face. "Monday night, you say. Yes, I remember that quite well because there was quite a ruckus going on up there."

"So he was home?" Jo asked.

Charlie shook his head. "No. That's the thing. He wasn't home. That was the problem--someone was knocking on his door and ringing the bell over and over, making a big racket for about ten minutes, but by the time I got up there to tell them he wasn't home, they had left."

"How did you know he wasn't home?"

"I'd seen him riding off on his bicycle about an hour before, and he didn't come back until after eight p.m."

"What time was this person knocking on his door?"

Charlie thought for a minute. "I'd say it must've been about six p.m. Wheel of Fortune was gonna be on in an hour, and I was getting my TV dinner ready so I could watch it. You know, I like the Salisbury steak--you know, the one with the corn and the little brownies."

Sam nodded. That was one of his favorites too. "And you're sure this was Monday night?"

"Oh sure, my memory's as good as gold." Charlie looked at Harry as if for confirmation, and Harry nodded.

"Charlie can still keep track of cards at poker night like nobody's business. And when we go to Vegas, well, you should see what happens. We come back with a lot of money."

Charlie smiled. Then the smile faltered, and he looked at Sam. "Not that I count cards or anything. That's illegal."

"Nothing illegal about having a good memory. And you're sure he didn't come back until eight p.m.?"

"Of course I'm sure. Didn't I say that?" Charlie seemed as if he was getting a little miffed.

"Do you know who was at his door?" Jo asked.

"That, I don't know. I didn't get up there right away because I was busy with my dinner. At first, I figured they'd go away when no one answered. But after a few minutes, I started up, but I was too late. They must have gone down the other stairway in back. I didn't see them, but whoever it was was knocking and ringing the bell as if they really wanted to get in and talk to him."

"And he was gone the whole time between six and eight?" Harry asked.

"Yes, sir, Chief--I mean ex-Chief," Charlie said.

Harry looked at Sam. "Well, there you go. That settles it. Sounds like we better talk to Brian, because right now he's at the top of my suspect list-- he had means, motive, and opportunity."

According to Charlie, Brian was at home, so they trudged up to the second floor and knocked on the door. Harry took the lead, pushing his way to the front, and Sam shot an amused look at Jo and shrugged. She knew what he was thinking--why not let the old guy have some fun.

Brian answered the door, gave Harry a confused look, and then saw Sam and Jo standing behind him. "Is there some news about my dad?"

Sam didn't think he looked guilty of trying to hide anything. He seemed genuinely concerned about his dad's case, but if that was true, why was he lying about where he'd been that night?

Sam's eyes drifted into the inside of the apartment. It was messy. An open pizza box on the table. Clothes strewn about. It smelled of dirty socks and stale food. Didn't Brian have a wife?

"May we come in?" Harry asked. "Is your wife home?" Apparently, Harry was thinking on the same lines as Sam.

Brian stepped back and opened the door. "My wife and I split up. That's why I'm living in the apartment. Who are you?"

Harry held out his hand. "Harry Woolston. Chief of police."

Brian frowned and looked at Sam.

"*Ex*-chief of police," Sam said. "Harry's helping us out."

"Okay. So what brings you guys here? I was just on my way to Mom's," Brian said.

"I think you might know why we're here," Sam said. "Do you know something about what happened to your dad?"

Brian's eyes darted around the room. "What do you mean? I told you I don't know anything."

"Really? Then why did you lie about being home the night he died?"

"I *was* home. Who said I wasn't?"

"Your landlord said you went out on your bike that night. You were gone for two hours. Long enough for you to cycle up to the cabin and back," Sam said. "Is that what you did?"

Brian sighed and sank into the sofa. "No. That's not where I was. But I did go out on my bike."

"Where did you go, and why on the bike?"

"I took my bike because I don't have a car. I got a DWI over in Pittsfield, and my license was yanked.

But my family doesn't know. I didn't want to tell them and worry my mom. She's going through so much already. And my sister has everything on her shoulders, so I didn't want to add to that. I wasn't lying because I was at the cabin. I was lying because I was in an AA meeting mandated because of the drunk driving charge. I had to take my bike because I lost my license." Brian looked up at Sam. "You can check with my sponsor."

Sam frowned. It could easily be checked, and Brian seemed sincere, but something didn't add up. "Really? Then why did your sister say she saw you moving around in here? Does someone else live here?"

Brian shrugged. "No one else was here, so I have no idea why she said that. I was just as surprised as you are. But I just kind of went with it so I wouldn't have to explain where I was. I figured maybe she got the night wrong or something. She's been really stressed out about Mom and running herself ragged to help out."

"She seemed pretty certain about the night she saw you."

Brian sighed again. "I don't know--she's my big sister and has always tried to protect me since we were little kids." He glanced at his phone on the table. "She's even trying to protect me with Mom's condition. Sugarcoating how bad it is, but asking me to come soon. I know why. Mom's getting a lot worse. And maybe she knew I was lying and wanted to corroborate my story? I'm sure she had good reason."

Sam looked at Jo. Maybe Melody hadn't lied to protect Brian--maybe she'd lied to protect herself.

CHAPTER TWENTY-EIGHT

As they left Brian's, Harry's phone blared with a loud foghorn sound, and he dug it out of his pocket. "Yes, Mable. Right away, dear. I'll be right home." He looked at Sam and Jo sheepishly. "Happy wife, happy life. Dang it! I'm gonna miss out on the interrogation of the sister. Can you drop me at the station? Do you need me to write down some questions for you to ask her, Sammy?"

"Thanks, I'm all set," Sam said.

They dropped Harry off and headed to Melody's. Her house was a neat little Cape in one of the newer sections of town. It had been built about ten years ago and was nicely kept up with a freshly mowed lawn, flowers, and neatly trimmed shrubs. Melody answered the door, the strain of her mother's illness evident in the tight set of her jaw. Or was it the strain of lying about her father?

"Is it about Dad?" She stepped back to let them in then led them toward the kitchen. "I've been at Mom's all morning and just came home for the break. She's fading fast."

Melody looked close to tears, and Sam felt bad that he was about to accuse her of killing her father. He didn't want to tell her Brian's secret, didn't feel right about being the one to let that out. He also wanted to play dumb so he could test the waters and see if she would still lie even if she knew she had been caught in it.

"I'm sorry to hear that. This won't take long. We have just a few things we want to tighten up in relation to your father."

"Okay. I really want to help you find out what happened. I still can't believe someone would kill him. Are you sure about that?"

"We can't rule it out," Sam said. "But there seems to be some kind of a question about the night he died. Are you sure you saw your brother at his place?"

Melody stiffened and turned away, busying herself with the teapot. "Coffee or tea?"

"No. We're good," Jo said. "Are you sure you saw your brother that night? We know you've been under a lot of strain, and you might've gotten the nights confused with everything that's going on."

Melody chewed her bottom lip. "If Brian said he was home, then he was home. I'm sure it was that night because I refilled Mom's prescription for her." Her brows knit together. "Or was it the night before when Mom wasn't home... she rarely goes out anymore and doesn't really have the energy to go in and out of the stores. Why are you asking?"

"We were just trying to verify where everyone was," Sam said.

"Well, I hope you don't think Brian was involved. He's just going through a rough patch right now."

"Honey, I put your bike away on the racks in the--" A man appeared in the doorway and stopped. "Oh, I didn't realize anyone was here."

"This is my husband, Joel," Melody introduced them. "They were just asking some questions about Dad's case." She turned back to Sam and Jo. "Anyway. I know Brian needs money. His wife left him, and he's gotten into a little bit of a mess, but he's a good guy."

"Maybe if your dad wasn't so tight with the money, Brian wouldn't be having any troubles," Joel said.

Melody turned on Joel. "That's not quite fair. Dad isn't a cheapskate. He just thought Brian should have to work things out for himself. Besides, Dad had his own problems."

"What do you mean?" Sam asked. Did Melody know about Tommy? But why would Tommy be a problem? Maybe she *did* know about the DNA test and thought Tommy was a problem for her father.

"Oh, well, just that there was a lot of stuff with Mom's medical treatments and doctor's appointments. You know insurance doesn't cover everything, and I've had to sort out the bills for them. Mom and Dad aren't getting any younger and can't handle all that." She glanced at the clock. "Really, I should go back. I don't like to leave my mother at all, and Brian was gonna meet me there. She was barely lucid when I left. The hospice nurse said there might not be much time, and I'd never forgive myself if I wasn't there when..."

Sam's heart pinched. This wasn't the time to be grilling Melody about her father's death, no matter what his suspicions were. The least he could do was let her tend to her mother's deathbed in peace.

"Of course." Sam started to the front door. "We'll be in touch if we have anything new."

"IT'S A TOUGH POSITION," Jo said when they were

back in the car. "Emotions are running high in that family, and it doesn't seem right to be accusing them when their mom is so sick."

Sam nodded. "You're right. We need to back off and let them take care of their mother. In the meantime, maybe we can reconstruct Mike's last day and check Brian's alibi for that night. Maybe we're barking up the wrong tree and no one in his family had anything to do with it. Maybe it really did have to do with Thorne," Sam said.

"But there's one thing that's bothered me. Mike was killed with his own gun. Only Margie, Mike, and the kids would have access to it and know the code to the lockbox. Now, we've assumed that Mike took it with him because he knew there would be trouble. But one of the kids could have brought it and killed him, hoping it would look like a suicide. They'd know he was depressed. Maybe Mike *didn't* bring the gun because he was expecting trouble with Thorne."

"Thorne was obviously interested in their land, but it doesn't add up. Why would he be paying Mike money and then kill him?" Jo asked.

"That brings up a good question. If the money wasn't from Thorne, where was it from?"

"Maybe he was selling something off? Or maybe he borrowed the money, knowing that he'd get something from Margie's life insurance," Jo said.

"I had Reese check into those life insurances, and there wasn't very much. The money was all in the value of the land that the farm is on." Sam's eyes narrowed as he turned down Main Street to the police station. "You might be on to something with him selling something off. At the Donnelly house, there was a china cabinet that was full of flow blue china. My grandma has some of that, and I know it can be worth a lot of money. And it seemed to me there were some empty spots in the Donnelly china cabinet."

Sam was really good at noticing details about various crime scenes. Jo didn't doubt he was right and his instincts were spot on about the china being missing. "But that doesn't really help us. If he was selling stuff off to give Tommy money, he was being sneaky about it so that the family wouldn't notice."

"Unless someone in the family *did* notice." Sam glanced over at her. "What if either Brian or Melody knew Mike was selling things off? What if they figured out he was up to something? What if they knew how the will was worded and realized that Mike had to die before Margie in order for them to be the only beneficiaries of the inheritance?"

"That's a great theory, but we need concrete evidence. Even if it was one of them, we're not about to go in and arrest them on Margie's deathbed," Jo said. "Maybe this would be a good time to slip in some footwork on Tyler's case." Jo tapped her finger against her mug. She thought it was a little strange that Sam hadn't mentioned much about Tyler's case since she'd found out about the twenty thousand, but maybe it was because they were busy working on Mike's.

Sam pulled into the parking spot in front of the police station. "We have to be careful about Tyler's case now, remember? Kevin mentioning the safety deposit box kinda spooked me."

Jo sensed him hesitate as he opened the car door. She got the impression that the post office box incident wasn't the only reason. Which was weird because Jo and Sam usually told each other everything... or so she thought.

But now, she had the distinct impression he was holding something back. Why did that feel like a betrayal?

Sam didn't owe her explanations for anything. They were colleagues, nothing more, and she knew from her own experience it was human nature for people to keep secrets from one another.

She hopped out and followed him into the police station. If Sam had something he wanted her to know, he'd tell her when he was ready.

CHAPTER TWENTY-NINE

In the station lobby, Reese was busy handing out yard sale permits to two old ladies. The women were perpetual yard salers—people that had yard sales all the time, practically making a business out of it. They'd pick things up at one sale then raise the price and put it in their own sale. He'd mentioned the limits on yard sales to them before.

He gave them a pointed glance, and one of them piped up. "This is only the third yard sale this year, and we're allowed five."

Sam tipped his head toward him. "That's right, ma'am. Make sure you don't overdo it."

He could see by the board that Kevin was out on a call. He felt bad that Kevin got all the minor calls, and he knew it bothered Kevin, but the truth was that Sam and Jo were the senior officers. Once they hired the new person, maybe he would let Kevin come on a few of the more interesting calls. Thoughts of the new hire made him anxious. He really should get going on interviewing. Maybe he would bring that last candidate back in and see what Jo thought of him.

Sam headed to the K-Cup machine and put a little orange-lidded container into the top then slid his dark-blue mug under the spout.

He could hear Jo in the corner, tapping her pencil on her desk, and his heart twisted. He knew Jo had sensed he wasn't telling her everything, and he hated that. But he couldn't tell her how he suspected Dupont knew what had happened twenty years ago. It wasn't something he was proud of, and besides, Mick was just as involved as Sam, so it wasn't only his story to tell.

But he could tell by the way she'd breezed past him and plopped down at her desk to stare at paperwork that her feelings were hurt. And for some reason that made him hurt, too. Why was that? It wasn't as if it were his duty to tell her every little thing--they were only co-workers, even though they were closer than most.

Lucy had come to press against him, as if sensing his sadness. He reached down and scrubbed the fur on top of her head with his fingertips. The dog was big enough that he didn't even have to bend down to pet her.

Sam sauntered into the squad room and rested his hip on the desk next to Jo. "I guess we need to prove that Tommy, Melody, and Brian couldn't have killed Mike because they were somewhere else. Tommy and Brian should be easy to prove if what they told us is true, but Melody... Maybe that won't be so easy."

Lucy whined and looked up at Sam then stuck her nose in the trash barrel.

"Are you feeding her enough?" Jo asked. "She looks like she's hungry."

Lucy gave a little whine and pushed harder, knocking the trash barrel over.

"I feed her plenty. I think Kevin and Dupont are spoiling her with those treats." Sam bent over to pick up the trash that had spilled out onto the floor. Lucy was sniffing at the pile, and as he bent to pick up the coffee receipt that had fallen out of Jo's jelly donut bag, Lucy slammed her paw down on it.

"Looks like she wants a donut," Sam joked. But as he tried to pull the receipt away, Lucy held steady. She looked up at him with her whisky-brown eyes as if to say, "Don't you get it?"

Sam looked down at the receipt, and a light bulb turned on in his head. "Wait a minute. This receipt gives me an idea. In the last case, we verified that one of the suspects couldn't have been a killer because he'd paid with a credit card at the gas station, and that gave him an alibi for the time of the murder. Maybe we can use receipts to prove what time Melody was at the pharmacy that night."

Jo shook her head. "I thought about that, but the pharmacy doesn't have receipts like that. They don't list the credit card name on the receipt like the gas station does." Jo reached over and tapped her pencil on the Brewed Awakening receipt that Sam was holding. "It's like this one that just has the time. It doesn't have a credit card number or note that it's a cash transaction, so we wouldn't be able to tell from the pharmacy receipt what time Melody picked up the prescription."

"That's only sort of true." Sam spun around to see Harry Woolston standing in the lobby. He didn't wait to be invited and just sauntered into the squad room as if they'd been expecting him. "You see, when you pick up pharmaceuticals, it's a whole different thing. There's privacy laws and HIPAA laws or whatever you call them. Anyway, whoever picks them up has to sign for it. So if your suspect was in the pharmacy picking up pills, then her signature would be recorded on the electronic signature gizmo, and I'm willing to bet it also records the time."

Sam didn't have much experience with the pharmacy, but it made sense. He pushed up from the desk and headed to the door. "Then I guess I better go make a visit over to the pharmacy right away."

"Don't worry. We'll wait here until you get back," Harry called after him as he rushed out the door.

THE PHARMACY WASN'T CROWDED, so Sam didn't have to wait in line. The pharmacist was Betsy Simmons, whom Sam had known since he was a kid. Her husband had left her two years ago, and she'd taken to flirting with Sam whenever they ran into each other. Sam wasn't in the mood for flirting, but if it helped him get the information he needed, then he'd play along.

Betsy looked up from under heavy black lashes. "Sam Mason, what can I do for you?"

Her tone and body language was suggestive, so Sam played into it. He leaned against the counter, rustling up the most charming smile he could muster.

"I was wondering if I could get some records about a prescription that was picked up here on Monday night." Normally, he'd have to get a court order for that, but maybe if he played his cards right, he could get the information he needed. If he needed the actual receipts, he'd go through the proper channels later, but for now it would help them to know exactly what time Melody picked up the prescription. That alone could knock her off the suspect list.

Betsy's eyes wavered uncertainly. "Well, I don't know..."

Sam leaned in closer and turned the charm up even higher. "I'd consider it a big personal favor."

"Well, I suppose it wouldn't hurt to say who came in that night. What exactly are you looking for?"

"You heard about Mike Donnelly..." Sam started.

Betsy's face turned sad. "Yes. Of course. Terrible thing."

"And you know Margie is very ill and gets a lot of prescriptions filled."

Betsy nodded. "She does. I feel terrible for their kids."

Sam nodded in sympathy. "On Monday night, Margie had a prescription filled by Melody, and I was just wondering if you could happen to look in there and see what time that was. I think it's all recorded in some database, right?"

Betsy perked up at the chance to show her knowledge. "Yes. It all has to be documented. When they come in to get the prescription, they have to sign for it. It's all recorded on the computer." She walked the length of the counter to a monitor and started typing. Her long fingernails clacked on the keys for a few seconds. Then she frowned. "Margie Donnelly, right?"

"That's right. But Melody came to get the prescription."

Betsy shook her head. "No, I don't think so."

"What do you mean?" Sam asked.

Betsy looked around the pharmacy to make sure no one else was near before she turned the screen so Sam could see it. She tapped a perfectly manicured nail on the signature. "Someone did pick up Margie's pills that night, but it wasn't Melody. It was Margie herself, and now I distinctly remember it because she was using that walker, and she could barely make it from the front door. It was sad because just a week earlier she didn't even need the walker."

Sam stared at the signature. If Margie had picked the pills up herself, then Melody had lied about being at the pharmacy the night her father was killed.

THEORIES CIRCLED like vultures in Sam's head as he drove back from the pharmacy. Either Melody had gotten her days mixed up, or she'd lied. What if instead of saying she was at the pharmacy and had seen Brian at home to cover for Brian, she was really trying to cover for herself? What reason would there have been to lie other than not wanting Sam to know where she was? Could she have been at the cabin? Did she know about Tommy? But how? Images of her holding the mail came to mind, and he wondered again to what address those DNA results had been mailed.

As he drove down Main Street, he passed Weatherby's antique store, and it hit him. Why hadn't he thought of it before?

If Mike had been selling the family china, what better place to do it then Weatherby's, and if one of his kids suspected, they might have gone to the store to find out.

Mike could have easily taken a few flow blue pieces out of the china cabinet. Margie would've been too sick to even notice they were missing. But Melody might have noticed.

He pulled over in front of the antique store and headed in. The bells over the large oak door tinkled as he stepped inside. Clara Weatherby smiled at him from behind the counter. Her snow-white hair and wrinkled face gave her a grandmotherly look, but Sam knew underneath she was a shrewd businesswoman.

"You ready to start that collection now?" Clara asked. She encouraged everyone in town to collect something. It was good for business, but it was also a fun hobby. She loved scouting around various antique stores, auctions, and estate sales to find just that perfect piece that someone could add to their collection.

Sam wasn't the collecting type. He had a cabin full of antiques and family heirlooms from his grandparents, which he treasured, but he was more of a minimalist himself. He didn't need a lot to make him happy. And, besides, most of his time was spent on the job, not sitting at home looking at a bunch of fancy collectibles.

"Not this time. I'm actually here on police business."

A perfectly plucked gray brow slid upward. "Oh?"

"I've got a suspicion that Mike Donnelly might've been selling off some of his family belongings."

Clara's eyes darted to a display case in the back of the room, and Sam saw the flow blue china in it. "Flow blue china, right?"

Clara nodded. "The pieces he had weren't that outstanding, not like the ones your grandma always refused to sell me. But with Margie being sick and all, I didn't have the heart to tell him, so I just paid him some money and let him bring them in. I figured he had bills. I know how expensive hospital stays and treatments can be."

"And was Mike the only one that knew about it?"

"I should say so. Margie would've been mad if she found out. The china had come down from her family. That's why I keep it back in there. I made the mistake of putting some in the window, and I nearly blew it."

"What do you mean?"

"It was about a month ago. Mike had been coming for about a month before that and bringing select pieces. Some of the flow blue, and he had some silver too." Clara glanced toward the big display window that looked out onto the main street. "I had put some of it in that window when I saw Margie and Melody pull up over across the way. That was back when Margie still got around pretty well. Anyway, I realized I made a big mistake. I didn't know Margie would be coming into town anymore, and if she saw that in the window, she'd flip. I didn't want to cause a problem with her and Mike, so I rushed over and took it out and put it in the case. I'd save it for her kids, but you know kids these days... they don't appreciate this old stuff. Better to sell it to someone who will be happy to own it."

"Did Margie or Melody see any of it that day?" Sam asked.

Clara sighed. "Thankfully not. I got it all out of the window before they came by, and they didn't come into the store, so I think I dodged a bullet there."

"And none of the family ever came in asking about it?"

"No. As far as I know, Mike's secret was safe from them."

Sam got back in the Tahoe and drove to the police station. What if Clara was wrong? What if Melody *had* seen the flow blue china and recognized it? On one of his visits to the Donnelly house, the china had been out on the dining room table, and Margie and Melody had been cleaning it. What if Melody recognized it in the store window from across the street and didn't want to upset her mother?

And what if she went to confront her father about it that night and discovered the truth?

CHAPTER THIRTY

Harry and Jo were still at the police station when Sam got back. Jo was filling out paperwork, and Harry was regaling Reese with tales of one of his investigative exploits.

Harry broke with Reese and trailed Sam back to the squad room area. "So what did you find out?"

Jo looked up, amused. "Yeah, what did you find out?"

Sam gave in. He needed to talk this out, and Harry wasn't going to leave. Besides, one more brain noodling on this might help.

"Melody lied. She didn't pick up the prescriptions from the pharmacy that night. Margie picked them up herself," Sam said.

Harry nodded sagely. "Interesting."

"Well, Brian and Tommy didn't lie." Jo leaned back

in her chair and put her feet up on the desk. "Both of their alibis checked out. They couldn't have killed Mike."

"Do you think Melody did it?" Harry asked.

Sam went over the corkboard where they'd pinned up all the information on the case. Notes, pictures, everything they had. Lucy followed and sat at his heels.

"Everything I've got is circumstantial. Just because she didn't pick up the medication at the pharmacy doesn't prove she was at the camp."

"What's her motive?" Harry asked.

"Mike was selling off family heirlooms to provide money for Tommy. Melody might have caught on to that. When we were at the house, I noticed some empty spaces in the china cabinet, and later on, Margie and Melody were cleaning that china. Melody might've noticed the pieces were missing."

"Her motive would be even stronger if she intercepted those DNA test results and knew she had a half brother that would inherit one-third of Mike's estate," Jo said.

"That would be motive enough given what was in the will," Harry said. "If Mike died before Margie, then only Melody and Brian would inherit. Mike's will gave everything to Margie, and Margie's will gave everything to her children, and Tommy wasn't one of her children."

"On the other hand, if Margie died first, which seemed inevitable, her wealth would go to Mike, but then when Mike died, everything would go to his issue. The three children. Melody and Brian would lose out on one-third of their inheritance," Jo said.

"But the Ritchies said they only ever saw the family cars at the camp that day. Mike's car was there, but maybe another family car was also there," Sam pointed out.

"Melody's car?" Harry asked.

"That's the thing. They didn't see Melody's car, just Mike and Margie Donnelly's cars. But their camp was past the Donnellys', so they wouldn't see everyone who visited the camp. They didn't even see the white Jetta, so we can't count that for anything."

Harry had taken a seat at the empty desk they had reserved for the new hire. He leaned back in his chair and looked up at Sam. "But Brian suggested Melody might've lied about going to the pharmacy to cover up for him. It seems plausible. And killing your dad because of an inheritance..." Harry shook his head. "I know that happens, but we're not talking that much money here, and it seems a little far-fetched given the case. Does she seem like the kind of crazy person that would do that?"

Sam shook his head and stared at the corkboard. "No. That's what's bugging me. It just doesn't add up."

Lucy whined and scratched at the wall underneath a picture of the Donnellys' driveway they'd taken the morning after the murder.

"The bicycle tracks!" Jo said. "When we were at Melody's, her husband said something about her bicycle."

Harry shook his head. "Why would Melody ride a bicycle all the way out there? Where does she live, and how long would it take her?"

"Well, she might've taken the bicycle so that nobody would see her car there. But she lives in the newer section of town, and that's a pretty far ride." Jo twisted her mouth and shook her head. "Maybe her husband did it. He didn't seem to like Mike very much."

"Or Brian. He rides a bicycle since he lost his license," Harry said.

Jo shook her head. "There wouldn't have been enough time to attend the AA meeting and cycle out to the camp."

Harry's eyes narrowed. "You think Melody knew about this other kid and told the husband, then he killed Mike so Melody wouldn't get gypped on her inheritance?"

"That doesn't seem likely. Sam's right. This doesn't add up. Even though she lied about being at the pharmacy, it might still have been to protect Brian. She's done that her whole life. And we don't know that she noticed the flow blue was gone or even found the DNA test results." Jo started digging through the pile of papers on her desk. "In fact, I have that DNA test right here. Maybe it says..." She whipped out a piece of paper with a red-and-gray logo. She frowned, then she held it up to Sam. "That letter didn't go to Mike's house. It went to Tommy, so if Melody knew about him, she didn't find out because of the bill."

Lucy whined and scratched again.

Sam looked closer at the picture, and suddenly, he knew what had been bugging him. "Shit. I don't think Melody was the killer. We've been barking up the wrong tree."

Harry leaned forward. "How so?"

"Look at this." Sam tapped on the picture. "I thought these bike tracks looked a little weird, but I assumed they were tracks that were coming and going. Now I see the spacing is too perfect. Too parallel. These aren't bike tracks--they're walker tracks."

Lucy's tail swished back and forth rapidly. "And now I remember, when we visited Margie those times, Lucy was very interested in sniffing the wheels on the walker. Lucy knew the whole time that it was Margie."

"So the tracks prove that Margie was there, but they don't prove that she killed Mike," Harry said. "She could have visited at any time. It was her camp, too."

"Not the tracks alone, but it all adds up," Sam said. "What if Margie knew Mike was selling off the flow blue and got suspicious? Mike had an affair with Tommy's mother seventeen years ago--do you think he could've hidden that from Margie? Wives know these things. Maybe she suspected the affair, but when Tommy's mother left, she might have thought she'd been wrong. I mean, she had her own family to think about, and with Tommy's mother gone, why pursue it?"

"Wait a minute! When we looked at that ATM footage of Mike getting the money from the ATM, the brown Taurus was on a side street. We thought Mike had driven it there, but he always drove the black truck. What if it was Margie in that car, spying on Mike?" Jo said.

"She might've figured out something was going on with Mike, and if she followed him and saw him meeting Tommy, she would know exactly why," Sam said. "Maybe she went to the camp and confronted him. At first, we had assumed Mike took the gun with him because he was expecting a fight, but what if it was Margie that brought the gun?"

"And now Margie is lying on her deathbed." Jo's eyes were dark with sympathy. "How can we go in and accuse a dying woman of murdering her husband?"

Sam sat in the chair and scrubbed his hands through his hair. "Good question. This would've been so much easier if Thorne was the killer."

Harry stood and clapped Sam on the shoulder. "Well, son, police chiefing doesn't always come easy. And now it sounds like you guys got yourselves a dilemma. In my experience, sometimes you have to choose between justice and doing the right thing. So what are you going to choose?"

CHAPTER THIRTY-ONE

S am and Jo stood at the Donnellys' front door with heavy hearts. He had a duty as chief of police to follow through on the investigation, but if his suspicions were correct, he didn't know what he was going to do about it. Still, he had to find out the truth. He had to hear from Margie's mouth if she was at the cabin that day. They still didn't have enough evidence to prove anything, but it all added up.

Melody answered the door, her eyes red and puffy.

"Come in." She sounded resigned as she held the door open.

"Mom's taken a drastic turn for the worse. The doctor said it won't be long now." She stood in the living room, her arms wrapped around her middle as she stared at Margie, lying in a hospital bed that had been set up near the window. Margie's breathing was shallow, her paper-thin skin as white as the sheets that were tucked around her.

Sam glanced at Jo. They wouldn't be getting a confession out of Margie now.

"I'm real sorry about that," Sam said.

Brian sat in the chair beside Margie, holding her frail hand. He nodded briefly at Sam and Jo and then moved his attention back to his mother.

Sam felt like an interloper. They had no business being there, even if it was part of their investigation.

"So have you found out what happened to my dad?" Melody asked.

"We're making progress. We just wanted to come and ask your mom a few questions, but..." Sam's voice drifted off. "We'll leave you alone now." He turned toward the door.

"Oh, wait..." Melody crossed the room to a small table and picked up a lilac-colored envelope. She handed it to Sam. His name was scrawled in shaky letters on the front.

"What's this?"

"Mom wrote it yesterday in one of her more lucid moments. She sealed it and made me swear not to look inside. Said if you came by to give it to you and for you to read it here."

Melody stepped back to her mother's side as Sam slid his finger under the flaps of the envelope. He pulled out a letter on matching lavender paper, written in the same shaky hand as his name on the envelope.

Jo looked over his shoulder as he read it.

CHIEF MASON,

YOU MIGHT HAVE ALREADY FIGURED this out. If not, I fear you are close. I know my time is near, and it won't do any harm to tell the truth. I want you to know for sure so you don't blame either of my kids... but maybe you'll take heart on a dying woman and not tell them. I don't want them to remember me as a monster.

I was the one that killed Mike. But the bastard deserved it. I knew about his affair with Judy Kendler all those years ago. But with two kids of my own, I chose to look the other way. And when she left town, I thought it was all in the past. Even when she returned a few years ago, I didn't catch on about her son.

But then shortly after she died, Mike started to act strange. Sneaking around. And that's when I noticed some of the family silver and flow blue china was missing. So I followed him one day and saw him meeting with that boy and giving him money. That's when I knew what he was up to.

I didn't have the time or energy to fight about it, but I figured Mike would try to include Tommy in everything, and I had to do something to protect my children's inheritance.

So I followed Mike to the cabin that night, and I shot the bastard with his own gun. Then I put the gun under him so it would look like he shot himself. Why couldn't you have just believed my suicide story? It would have been better for all if you had. But now that you seem hell bent on investigating, I'm afraid you might misinterpret the clues and accuse Melody or Brian. So I leave you with this confession. It's up to you what you do with it.

SINCERELY,

Margie Donnelly

SAM WAS HOLDING the confession for Mike Donnelly's murder in his hand, but it didn't make him feel as if justice had been served. What was he going to do now? Arrest a dying woman?

He glanced up at Melody and Brian, bending over their mother, their faces creased with grief. Neither one of them had had anything to do with this, and apparently, neither one of them knew about Tommy. What good would come of making it known that their mother had killed their father? It would only add to their despair. Harry's words about choosing between justice and doing the right thing came back to him. Mike's killer was getting a worse punishment than any normal course of justice would bring.

Melody looked up at him, her brows tugging together. "What was in the letter? Anything important?"

Sam tapped the letter against his leg. He glanced at Jo. They didn't need to exchange words. He knew she was totally on board with what he was about to do. "Kind of. It lays to rest some of the questions we had about your father's death."

Brian jerked his head up. "You know who did it?"

"Well, that's the thing. Turns out your mom was right in the first place. She said your dad was very upset about her prognosis. But because the vultures had contaminated the crime scene, we got some of the evidence wrong. Nobody killed your dad. He killed himself."

The looks of relief on their faces were worth it. They'd already come to terms with their father's death, and having it be ruled a suicide as opposed to murder was actually much easier for them to deal with now, especially when the murderer was their own mother. Sam didn't know what he was going to do to persuade the medical examiner to look at the evidence in such a way that it could be ruled a suicide. It wasn't as if they had evidence to the contrary--it was simply that the vulture damage had made it impossible to get the evidence they needed to prove it was a suicide. Sam knew he could finagle things to get the verdict he needed.

Margie sighed. Her eyes fluttered but didn't open. It was as if it were a sign that Sam had done the right thing. Sam and Jo turned toward the door. "We'll leave you alone now. Sorry for your losses."

CHAPTER THIRTY-TWO

Three days later...

HOLY SPIRITS WAS CROWDED for a Monday night. Sam and Jo sat at the bar and ordered the usual.

"Here's to a job well done." Sam tipped his beer bottle toward Jo's, and they clanked the rims together.

Sam had managed to complete the investigation in a way that proved it was a suicide. He had the vultures to thank for that. They'd damaged the body in such a way that any of the usual indications that it was suicide, such as angle of entry and powder on the hands, were inconclusive. Since Sam's investigation hadn't turned up anyone that had means, motive, and opportunity, no one argued when the case was closed as a suicide.

Margie had died the day before, and Sam doubted anyone would have even believed she could have made it out to the cabin, much less shot her husband, even if he'd tried to bring a case against her.

"It's all working out for the best." Jo nodded toward the table in the corner where Tommy was hesitantly approaching Melody and Brian. There was a short, awkward conversation, and then Melody stood and pulled Tommy into a hug, Brian stood and shook his hand, then the three of them sat down at the table.

"They lost two parents so close, but they gained a brother," Sam said.

Kevin slid into a chair next to Sam. He was also watching the Donnelly table. "Isn't that the kid that Mike Donnelly was giving money to sitting with his other kids?"

"Yep," Sam said.

"How did they know about him? I thought you weren't going to say anything," Kevin said.

"Didn't have to." Sam took a sip of beer and swung back around to face the bar. "Turns out Melody already knew about him. She'd seen the china at the antique store and knew her father was up to something. She followed him and saw him meeting Tommy. She knew who Tommy was. She was fifteen when Mike had the affair with Judy, and that was plenty old enough to know what was going on."

"Huh." Kevin looked over his shoulder, and Sam followed his gaze. The three of them were laughing, and the sight warmed Sam's heart.

Kevin frowned. "Wait a minute. Then she might have had a good reason to kill her father. And we know she lied about being at the pharmacy..."

"True," Sam said. He and Jo had burned Margie's confession letter after they'd left the Donnellys' that day. Neither of them had any intention of telling anyone else about it. "But it turns out she had an alibi. She was the one that was knocking on Brian's door the night Mike was shot. She'd just figured out what was going on with Tommy and went to Brian's to tell him. Turns out one of the nosey neighbors saw her and can verify."

"That's why she acted so funny when we asked about their whereabouts and Brian lied about being home. She knew he wasn't there because she'd been knocking on his door. She had no idea about the AA meeting, so she made up the story about seeing him from the pharmacy to protect him," Jo added.

"Wow, I guess sometimes family really does stick

together." Kevin finished his beer and stood. "Well, gotta get home. See you guys tomorrow."

The sound of rustling paper came from Jo's direction as Sam watched Kevin walk away. He turned to see her staring at some kind of pamphlet. "What is that?"

She held the front up to reveal a black-and-white picture of a rectangular fish tank. "Finn's getting a little cramped in his fish bowl, and the guy at the pet store said that a regular tank with a filter would be much healthier for him, so I bought him this tank a few days ago. Gotta figure out how to set it up. Maybe I can even get him a few friends."

"So Finn's putting down roots. Gonna be staying a while?" Sam looked at Jo carefully. Though she'd been here for four years, he'd always sensed that she might pick up and leave at any time. The thought made him feel empty, and he realized for the first time how important she'd become to him. And not just at work, either.

"Yeah, well, if I can figure this out. There's a lot to it, with gravel and filters and some kind of water cycling thing you have to do." Jo flipped through the pages. The pamphlet was thick with instructions.

"Maybe I could come over and help you out. I could bring Lucy and introduce her to Finn." Sam said it casually, even though his pulse was racing. He and Jo didn't usually hang out at each other's houses. Their social activities were usually confined to having a beer after work at Holy Spirits. He sensed that going over to her house to help her set up the tank would be a step in another direction. Or was he making too much of it? It was just setting up a fish tank, for crying out loud.

Jo kept staring at the pamphlet. Was she avoiding eye contact?

"That would be great," she said.

She looked over the top of the pamphlet at the Donnelly table. The three of them were laughing and enjoying themselves. Jo smiled. "Sometimes something good can come from something bad."

Sam glanced over. "Yeah..." Something beyond the table caught Sam's eye. Someone walking into the bar with an arrogant swagger. Someone he didn't want to see. Thorne. "Oh shit."

"What?" Jo's eyes narrowed, then she made a face when she saw Thorne. "Oh."

Thorne came straight to the bar and pushed his way in between them, facing Sam and with his back to Jo. Sam imagined Jo was probably relieved not to have to talk to him. He was standing too close for comfort, and Sam could smell sickly spicy aftershave.

"I have something you might want to see, Mason," Thorne said in a low voice as he leaned even closer and pulled a plastic bag out of his front pocket.

Sam's eyes fell on the bag that Thorne was dangling in front of him. A jolt of shock nearly knocked him off his chair as the bar lighting glinted off the stainless-steel pocketknife. He recognized it as Mick's knife, one he'd lost a long time ago. But how had Thorne ended up with it, and what was that dark stain on the side?

His eyes flicked up to Thorne's. Dark and beady with a smug hint of superiority. Thorne had been shielding the knife from view of anyone else. "That's right. You recognize that, don't you? That's the knife you and your friend used years ago. The knife that might reopen a murder investigation. So, if I were you, I'd think twice about harassing me, and back off on Dupont while you're at it. He and I have big plans for this town."

Thorne shoved the knife back into his pocket, spun, and walked out just as quickly as he'd come in, leaving Sam staring out into the bar with a sinking sensation in his stomach.

"What was that about?" Jo asked.

"Nothing, just Thorne and his usual hot air. Nothing to worry about." Sam faked a smile but avoided Jo's eyes. He was afraid that if he looked at her, she'd know he was lying. Because despite his dismissive words, deep down inside, Sam was very, very worried.

****

WHAT IS THORNE UP TO? Find out more in Book 3 - Exposing Truths:

Exposing Truths (Book 3)

JOIN my readers list to get new release notifications:
https://ladobbsreaders.gr8.com

DID you know that I write mysteries under other names? Join the LDobbs reader group on Facebook on find out! It's a fun group where I give out inside scoops on my books and we talk about reading!

https://www.facebook.com/groups/ldobbsreaders

ALSO BY L. A. DOBBS

Sam Mason Mysteries

***

Telling Lies (Book 1)

Keeping Secrets (Book 2)

Exposing Truths (Book 3)

Betraying Trust (Book 4)

Killing Dreams (Book 5)

Crossing Lines (Book 6)

More books in the Rockford Security Series:

Cold As Her Heart

A Game of Kill

No One To Trust

No Time To Run

Don't Fear The Truth

Hide From The Past

ABOUT THE AUTHOR

L. A. Dobbs also writes light mysteries as USA Today Bestselling author Leighann Dobbs. Lee has had a passion for reading since she was old enough to hold a book, but she didn't put pen to paper until much later in life. After a twenty-year career as a software engineer, she realized you can't make a living reading books, so she tried her hand at writing them and discovered she had a passion for that, too! She lives in New Hampshire with her husband, Bruce, their trusty Chihuahua mix, Mojo, and beautiful rescue cat, Kitty.

Her book "Dead Wrong" won the "Best Mystery Romance" award at the 2014 Indie Romance Convention.

Her book "Ghostly Paws" was the 2015 Chanticleer Mystery & Mayhem First Place category winner in the Animal Mystery category.

Join her VIP Readers group on Facebook:

https://www.facebook.com/groups/ldobbsreaders

Find out about her L. A. Dobbs Mysteries at:
http://www.ladobbs.com

This is a work of fiction.

None of it is real. All names, places, and events are products of the author's imagination. Any resemblance to real names, places, or events are purely coincidental, and should not be construed as being real.

CPSIA information can be obtained
at www.ICGtesting.com
Printed in the USA
LVHW040126091020
668359LV00013B/697